The FEAR of MONCROIX

BRYAN ASHER

Other Novels
by
Bryan Asher

The Assassin of Malcoze

The Treasure of Lor-Rev

INTERCONT PRESS

The Fear of Moncroix

Illustrations Copyright © 2023 by Bryan Asher

Written by Bryan Asher

Cover Illustration by Christian Angel

Character Illustrations by Christian Angel

Cover Design by Elizabeth Mackey

Chapter Header Illustrations from Canva's free use collection

This book is published through Intercont Press LLC

ISBN 978-1-7357628-4-5 (Paperback)

ISBN 978-1-7357628-5-2 (eBook)

www.intercontpress.com

www.ashernovels.com

To Kevin, Andy & Jordan,

Without you all, I may never have gotten these books off the ground.

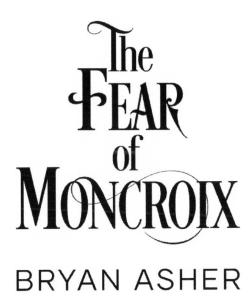

The FEAR of MONCROIX

BRYAN ASHER

PROLOGUE

HE BRISKLY LEAPED from tree to tree, careful not to let himself slip from the high resting branches. Falling was not an option, as the murky bogs of this forest were filled with grimy substances not meant for mortals to bathe in. Davion had been practicing his skills as a Wayward for decades; aerial travel was a commonplace feat for someone in his order. His destination, however, was anything but. He'd received a summons of high importance from the longstanding steward of the Waywards, Gerine Mathiss. While not retaining a strict bureaucratic structure, the most tenured individual within their calling was responsible for disseminating vital information. Tonight's summoning was only used by Gerine for items of grave concern. In all his years serving, Davion had only received one prior to tonight's gathering.

His violet eyes squinted through the darkness. Despite only having a faint teal moonlight to assist his vision, his enhanced senses noticed the trees thinning ahead. His pace slowed while reaching the last branch before the clearing. Taking notice of the circular grass field below, he saw several of his colleagues had already arrived. Stepping off the branch, the back of his overcoat flapped furiously as he plummeted towards the ground, some twenty feet below. As his toes touched the grass blades, Davion tucked one shoulder and rolled gracefully into a perfect landing. As he approached the group, another attendee, Celiss Wile, turned to greet Davion with a familiar grin.

"So, what did I miss, Celiss?" Davion asked while brushing his black hair away from his eyes.

"Only a bit of chatter. Nothing formal has been mentioned," his friend answered.

Davion tilted his head quizzically. "No one here has any inclination why Mathiss called this meeting? Not even a word from Alucore or Christovelle? They're always lingering around Central Grounds."

Celiss bit his inner cheek and shook his head. "I'm afraid not. Even the most connected have no idea."

Davion glanced at the other members, scanning their faces for signs someone was clued in. All in attendance had crossed arms, hunched shoulders, or furrowed brows. Everyone he saw was guarded and poking around for answers, just like himself. Breathing deeply, he decided to abandon his query until Mathiss arrived.

"Since we've got time to spare, we might as well share a drink," Davion said while unclasping the top flap of his hip pouch.

Since he was traveling deep into the Tainted Bog, Davion packed light, only bringing one pouch for each hip and two daggers. He retrieved a small silver flask etched with an intricate design of two wolves and a mountain.

"I got this from a tavern in the south, just outside Wolven territory," Davion said before taking a swig.

He bit his lip and exhaled sharply after finishing his sip, then handed the flask to his friend, "Surprisingly smooth for a spirit crafted by Werewolves."

Celiss inspected the flask as he turned it over in his hand, then cocked an eye at Davion. "I've heard Turn-skins make the best rum, but I've yet to taste it."

Celiss blinked and shook his head after taking a pull from the silver flask. "Smooth on the outset, yes, but it definitely has some bite."

Davion nodded in agreement as he accepted the drink back from his companion.

"Mind if I snag a pinch," a gruff voice called out.

He extended the flask to the approaching man, whose hefty frame and bald scalp contrasted the thin features and long hair of Davion and Celiss.

"Sure, Harald," Davion replied while handing it over.

He noticed some new black markings lining the side of Harald's scalp.

"Is that fresh ink there, friend?" Davion asked.

Harald grunted and traced a sausage-like finger over the newest tattoo on his skull. It was a sequence of jagged lines that blended with the other ones.

"I had this added after my last encounter. I fought a unique ghoul that sprouted wings..."

"Ghouls don't have wings," Celiss interrupted.

Harald shook his head, waving a hand. "I know that, Celiss, but this truly was a mutated ghoul. I'm certain because it maintained its shape after it was slain. I honestly wondered if this

9

meeting might be related to that. If we're all discovering new mutations from different creatures, it could have wider implications for Moncroix."

Celiss held an unconvinced stare but avoided objecting any further. He whipped the sides of his long, deep-blue overcoat behind him before stuffing his hands into his trouser pockets. Davion secured the flask into his pouch and adjusted his shirt, then knelt to fix the straps on his tall leather boots. While he could easily traverse the treetops surrounding this swamp, it gave his clothes a light beating.

The center of the field began quivering slightly, and everyone stepped back into a semi-circle around it. The quaking ground shook once more before the earth rose into a spherical clump. The grass and dirt shed away to reveal a new attendee... Gerine Mathiss had arrived.

A circular pattern of woven lines made with soft jade light rested at his feet. Their pulsating glow pulled the terrain back together, returning the earth to its original state. Gerine was the only member skilled enough in spellcraft to create a transportation ring. One hand could sufficiently count the remaining capable casters occupying their nation. As he stood in the circle to collect himself, everyone watched his figure intently. His head was bowed, thick strands of white hair covering his face from view. His long blue overcoat, lined with white and gold trim, glinted off the faint light of his spell.

Raising his head slowly, he met the watchful eyes of those surrounding him. He noted that there wasn't a single Wayward inhabiting the Intercontinent of Moncroix who wasn't in attendance. Of all the floating nations encompassing the Intercontinental Forum, theirs was the most peculiar. Anyone who traveled here by airship likely visited the substantial city of Qulàire. A sprawling capital that allowed visitors but walled itself off from the rest of its homeland, and for good reason.

The majority of Moncroix outside its stone wall was claimed by clusters of afflicted people and roaming monsters. The three largest territories being Halnoth, occupied by the Wolven; the Tainted Bog, housing many Witches; and Vèspige, claimed by the Vampires. The remaining land between their territories was occupied by a smattering of quaint towns and small villages run by unafflicted humans.

Everyone referred to it unofficially as the Midland. Some towns in this area were fortunate enough to have a witch or warlock residing within, which staved off most monsters. While ghouls, bloodsuckers, and turn-skins occasionally hunted nearby towns, they would never cross one inhabited by a powerful magician. The only other source of protection for those residing in the ungoverned Midland was the Waywards. Traveling legionnaires who bound themselves to the magical spirits resting within their homeland, they used that given power to provide justice for those incapable of protecting themselves.

Gerine stepped forward from his casting and took a scroll from his belt. "I require a complete majority to enact this proclamation," he stated firmly, holding it aloft.

Davion elbowed Celiss. "How can he expect a complete majority?!"

Celiss shook his head. "No idea. I can count on one hand how many times we've even reached a dominant majority," he whispered under his breath.

Davion nodded in agreement, continuing to stare forward.

Gerine clenched his right fist and turned it. As he did so, the same ring of lines from his transportation spell circled his wrist. It was the sign of their Wayward power, the symbol of their bond to the spirits within the Midland. A power you could only wield beyond Qulàire's wall. Those who tried to leave Moncroix with this magic had their vessels scattered to a thousand pieces. A fate the afflicted monsters also suffered from; their wrists encircled by magical Snares as well.

"If any of you do not wish to enact this proclamation, I'll give you this chance to break your bonds and leave the Midland," he said while the magic pulsated around his wrist. "This is something so dire we cannot hesitate."

Everyone's murmuring hushed. No steward of their order had ever suggested this.

"I've been given notice on good authority that a group of Vampires is close to leaving this Intercontinent," Gerine continued.

"Impossible…" a voice interjected. "There's no chance they've circumvented the Spirit's Snare."

Gerine turned to meet the man. He wore a dark brown coat that reached his waist. Small gold spikes covered his shoulders and went down the back of his jacket, creating an intricate pattern of a lion baring its teeth.

"I have strong connections who speak with the Royal Vampiric Court, and I've heard no word of this."

"My source is closely linked as well," Gerine stated flatly while pointing the scroll back at him. "They discovered one of their sisters trying to improve a potion allowing them to go beyond the Spirit's reach. One of their own already used it to walk inside Qulàire's walls briefly. Until the Spirits yanked them back."

Luke – one of the more experienced members – shook his head. "This seems suspicious..."

"I assure you it's real. He was pulled through the front gate. Qulàire guardsmen found the diced remains just outside the silver bars. When they found the teeth – in what was left of the corpse – they contacted me to assist with their investigation."

Luke pursed his lips and resisted further comment. Silver was the metal of weakness for anyone Snared.

Another Wayward stepped forward; his slender frame and delicate features were blanketed by a long overcoat covered in tiny, jagged stones. "If the Vampires already have this potion, why would this person wait until now to alert us?" Regus asked.

Gerine nodded. "As I stated earlier, it's not the one directly responsible. Only recently, they were made aware after being recruited to assist in its development. They're worried this magic would allow the Vampiric Court to rule the entirety of Moncroix."

Regus scoffed at his reply. "Of course. They want us to clean this mess off the floor like dogs licking scraps. Hoping we can deal with the Vampire rather than doing it themselves."

Gerine raised a finger as he spoke. "I understand how this may seem, but this is a legitimate magical concoction. We all know that the Snare keeps you from reaching beyond the wall. Only Snared humans have successfully broken their bonds but, in doing so, have lost their magical enhancements. If their improvements continue, these Vampires could craft something that lets them not only walk into Qulàire..." Gerine paused and bit his lower lip, "but the other nations beyond Moncroix."

13

Regus observed him with a deep frown. "And who's to say this potion can be improved upon. Maybe its pinnacle has been reached?"

Gerine stared back at him confidently. "I've brought proof."

His last words bathed the gathering in silence. Gerine motioned towards a thick patch of mighty trees behind several men. The group turned their heads as a Witch shuffled forward. Raising her eyes to survey the group, her forehead curled into several rolls. Her face was a mixture of chubby wrinkles and sagging skin, and her cheeks hung like a butcher's strung-up cutlets. She shot a hand from her cloak and revealed a corked oval glass vial that came to a point on its bottom. The attending Waywards stared intently as she placed it into Gerine's outstretched palm.

"This version," he said, holding the vial between two fingers, "allows a Snared user to obtain the properties of a Vampire. Do you doubt – with continued research – that this concoction could eventually mask them long enough to flee Moncroix or potentially hide their Snare and retain its power?"

Hushed chatter clambered around Gerine. He held his tongue until they were finished.

"Peregrine here has obtained this from another of her sisterhood. She can make enough vials for us to infiltrate the Royal Vampiric Court," Gerine stated while placing the potion in one of his coat's outer pockets. "So far, I've uncovered very little about who is ultimately funding this magical research. Witches willingly share recipes, but not who purchases them," he continued, shaking his head. "At the pace it's progressing, I'm fearful they'll reach their goal by next harvest," he paused to walk about the circle, eyeing each of his colleagues directly. "The only way I see us dealing with this threat is banding together to sneak inside their ranks and remove whoever is responsible."

A pregnant pause fell over the gathering, and Gerine looked about them to see who would step forward first.

Davion glanced down at his wrist, turning it to reveal his Spiritual Bond. The circle of light-blue waving lines danced around his arm. Should he break these bonds? Were the Waywards truly meant for organized espionage, especially within as powerful a bureaucratic structure as the Royal Vampires? The friend to his left stepped forward...

"I vote to join. I agree with Gerine. If this is left unchecked, there won't be a Midland for us to protect," Celiss firmly stated.

The man to Davion's right also moved forward but twisted his wrist to reveal his magical crest.

"I don't believe the Waywards were built to interfere in the political matters of Vampires," Harald said.

"I second that," Luke interjected while revealing his Snare, "This group was started as a means of justice for those we come across in our travels. I joined the Waywards because we agreed to share knowledge and maintain a set of ideals while protecting the powerless. I don't believe we're a secret society, deeming itself righteous enough to decide the fate of this Intercontinent from the shadows," Luke turned to face a few of his comrades, "If that means I must break my bonds to the Spirits... then shatter this magic and I'll find life without this order."

Gerine bit his lip and lifted his chin, keeping himself from interrupting. He desperately needed everyone he could

15

corral to fend off this threat but jumping into the verbal fray now would appear desperate rather than persuasive.

A small cluster across from Davion ventured forward. "I agree with Gerine. We swore an oath to act upon the evils that prey on our homeland. While it's beyond our initial approach to these threats, we can't stand by and do nothing with this information."

Davion took another solid breath while contemplating the implications. Vampires were very dangerous creatures but completely untested beyond their kingdom of Vèspige. No one had seen what lengths their power could reach while inhabiting a larger Intercontinent like Malcozé or Kratas. He'd even heard rumors there were some in the nation of Lor-Rev who mimicked their culture and appearance. Going so far as sharpening their own teeth.

If the Vampires were to escape, they could only act at nightfall, which might curb a great deal of their ambition. Yet, he'd fought one firsthand. Their ability and fiendish nature brought him the toughest fight of his tenure. If that was only one, imagine what the organized Court could achieve. He pondered the havoc it had caused to that small village before he arrived to save them.

Davion stared at the circular magic he'd obtained as a Wayward, still swirling around his wrist. He swallowed the lump in his throat and searched his soul for answers. Did he stand up to this impending threat, or was this best left for someone else?

He took one last breath before stepping forward... then raised his arm in favor of infiltrating the Royal Vampiric Court.

CHAPTER ONE

THE HALLWAY WASN'T the common size of most within House Malnuvious. Davion observed the white brick on either side, noticing this section was narrower. Peering ahead, he saw a slim figure watching him. His eyes wouldn't have caught the shrouded man if not for the flames of candlelight dancing in nearby sconces. He tried calling out, but his jaw seemingly fought back against the thought. The walls started curling around him, causing Davion to recklessly charge ahead. Reaching the end of the hallway, he tumbled forward, rolling across the marble floor and landing at the feet of the mysterious figure.

He looked up and saw Celiss smiling over him. Not a comforting one, but a toothy, fiendish grin. Davion climbed to his feet and grabbed his friend's shoulders. More attempts at speech were fruitless, his words captured in the base of his throat. The shoulders he held melted between his fingers as his friend sank to the cold floor in a pile of gnarled clothing. He clawed feverishly at the puddle of clothes before him, but nothing remained within the fabric...

Davion lurched upright from his dream, seated on his bed. After a pair of heavy breaths, he wiped his brow and leaned back against the walnut headboard.

How long had it been since he last had that dream? Five years... maybe more? Close to a decade had passed since all the Waywards were murdered by the Vampires. All except him. After their plan was uncovered during a Royal gala, he'd barely survived that slaughter. Celiss was the only reason he'd left that ballroom with his throat unscathed.

He'd initially tried to discover which Royal laid the trap for his order. After two years of downing the potion to masquerade as a Vampire and exhausting every possible lead, he'd found nothing substantial. When that failed, he looked to untether his Snare and flee Moncroix. Unfortunately, the only person with the knowledge to do so was Gerine, who was dead now. Any plans of revenge or escape were buried in the dirt with his lost brethren.

He looked to the other side of his bed at the woman who shared his resting quarters. Observing her, he couldn't help but notice that her flowing crimson hair mirrored the spilt human blood from the regal banquet they'd attended last night.

'*Celiss, if you only knew what I'd become, I don't think you'd have saved me...*' Davion pondered.

He wrapped himself in a long robe woven from black silk and stepped towards his changing room.

A feminine voice called out behind him, "Leaving so soon, Davion."

He turned to face her, Viscountess Adelina Mayjere. She currently occupied one station above his own and belonged to a very prestigious family. Their relationship wasn't one of lengthy courting; rather, they occasionally joined one another after noble events.

"I have an appointment with Duke Roycen. You know he likes to meet just before sunrise," Davion answered.

She rolled her eyes. "The inconvenience of having humans maintain those farms, I suppose. Please visit before the next gala, Davion."

He gave a deep nod that was one step away from bowing, then took his leave.

Stepping through the stone archway, Davion headed towards the gravel path surrounding the grounds. Most within the nobility would ask to be driven. He didn't feel like waiting for someone to bring him a carriage, nor did he feel like enduring the customary chit-chat the vessel's driver would likely bring, not after dreaming of his dead friend.

His boots crunched across the tiny rocks towards the stables. The only downside of driving himself was that he had to collect his own horse, or Horslich, as they were called after being bound to Vampiric magic. He hated setting foot in the stables. These weren't your standard dapples and greys but other beasts entirely. The creatures inhabiting this wood structure were once considered horses, but now they resembled something ghoulish. Bonded to the Spirits and afflicted with the same magic as their masters, their tongues now hung from the side of their mouths while beady red pupils gazed forward soullessly. Somehow the sophistication of their owners wasn't passed down after binding. However, their unending stamina and lack of hunger or thirst made them invaluable.

19

He snatched the reins of the nearest one and marched it towards an unoccupied carriage. He lifted his left arm and turned, displaying his own magical crest. His normal light-blue circle had red lines swirling inside, the sign of Vampiric power. Initially, he was amazed that the Witches' tonic not only endowed him with their physical attributes but added the additional lines within. After years of hiding within the royal ranks, it felt natural now.

Subsequently, a circle mimicking Davion's Snare hovered around the beast's neck. It obeyed his thoughts and trotted towards the front of the carriage with an odd gait that rhythmically matched a limping corpse. After leashing it to the front, he climbed inside the carriage and closed his eyes. He envisioned his destination and how to get there, guiding the bonded beast.

He imagined the one-story, blue ranch house with white trim, which sat on a vast farm several miles from his current whereabouts. After his thoughts concluded, the carriage jolted forward and rushed along the path at a dizzying pace. The beasts may have walked like haggard remnants of their former selves, but the magic within enhanced their gallop.

Duke Roycen was one of the few humans the Vampiric Court allowed to hold a position of power. There were only a few of them, and they secretly ran the larger settlements far from the Royal's stately castles. The Dukes appeared to be leaders of prosperous cities, but in actuality, they were running little more than breeding grounds for the Vampire's feasts.

'The inconvenience of having humans maintain those farms.'

Adelina's words were strung up and hung before his mind. He tried to ignore the implications of his former order losing that fight. How Celiss had done everything to save him, and now he was an accomplice to the Vampire's vision for the Midland. The Waywards' loss had more immediate consequences than walking beyond the Snare. That was another hunt he'd given up on. After that fateful gala, he tried to uncover more about the rumors of evading the Spirit's grasp, yet reached the same dead ends.

'Maybe they realized it was an impossible task and just gave up,' he thought, *'or it was just concocted to lay a proper trap.'*

Peering through a set of thick black curtains, Davion saw the Duke's home in the distance. Out of all the humans working in concert with the Court, Duke Roycen was his favorite. He was a blunt man who somehow maintained a steady calmness despite the swirl of regal monsters overruling his decisions.

"I see you came without a driver again," Roycen said while standing on his front porch. He wore pleated olive-colored trousers connected to a set of brown suspenders resting over his white button-front shirt. Despite the humble attire, his ability to lead was never questioned.

"I prefer to arrive unmonitored. There are enough leering eyes within the castles," Davion answered while ascending the wide wooden steps.

Roycen leaned on the porch railing near him, holding a thin stick in his other hand. He twisted it back and forth absentmindedly while staring out towards a large wheat field.

"What brings you here, Davion?" Roycen asked.

"I have a letter from Count Viruticus. He requests a hunt within one of your settlements," Davion answered, retrieving a sealed envelope from his black overcoat.

Roycen turned his head slightly in acknowledgment but didn't make eye contact. His long-brim hat cast an odd shadow across his face that kept Davion from reading him. He wondered if the idea of ruling these people like cattle ever wore on Roycen, even though his calmness showed the same indifference Davion had acquired.

Roycen finally answered, "Which land?"

Davion nodded to the letter in his outstretched hand.

Roycen raised an eyebrow. "If you're making me open that letter, I'm guessing I won't like what's written on it."

Davion remained silent, leaving his hand outstretched.

Roycen tore open the envelope and shook his head upon reading its contents.

He held up the letter and shook it once. "I've told House Viruticus that back-to-back hunts in the same town will make people wise. You must keep hunts spread out and random."

He observed Davion, who only returned his glare with a weak frown in agreement. Roycen pursed his lips and rubbed his thin moustache with his forefinger and thumb.

"It's his son, Thadric, isn't it?" he asked, "The spoiled brat wants to hunt Gilhem again."

Davion nodded. "After this one, however, Count Viruticus assured me it will be the last hunt there for at least two years."

Roycen nodded. "Good. It'll take some time for those people to recover after that boy and his lot tear that village to shreds."

Davion licked his fangs absentmindedly and walked towards the double doors of Roycen's home.

"Any chance you'd host me in the cellar for some wine?" he asked, gesturing towards the green shard stabbed into the wood above Roycen's door.

The Snare placed upon Vampires wouldn't allow them into any homes appropriately marked without the owner's consent. A commoner was required to write a specific spell of particular ingredients over their doors that lasted only a few hours. However, someone of Duke Roycen's wealth could procure an expensive gem enchanted by a Witch or Warlock, which held the spell indefinitely. He didn't truly need one since none of the Court would suck the blood of an appointed human. It was merely a measure of appearing on the same side as any human visitors.

Roycen led the way and opened the door for Davion. "It always surprises me that you stay with House Viruticus. They're so gaudy and flamboyant."

"I'd argue I fit in just fine," Davion replied.

"Spare me the Royally appropriate answer," Roycen replied, "We both know you're more level-headed than that dramatic family."

"Not every member of a House fits the exact mold of its leaders," Davion replied while glancing out the nearest window. It was almost daybreak.

"The better you fit in with a House, Davion, the higher you ascend," Roycen replied.

"Ascend..." Davion answered while approaching the dark staircase leading to Duke Roycen's wine cellar, "I'm afraid that's not in the cards for me anymore. I'm happy to explain more over a glass of wine."

Roycen smirked at his remark. "Well, you're obviously welcome to share one with me before I leave. I'll draw the curtains on my way out. You can rest here until nightfall."

Davion patted him thankfully on the shoulder before descending the stone steps to the cold, sunless room, which mirrored his existence for the last decade. He hoped sharing a few glasses of Carménère with Roycen would dull the painful reminder of Celiss, constantly clawing to the forefront of his thoughts.

CHAPTER TWO

CRIES OF AGONY erupted from the fanged mouth as a thin rapier sword plunged through the Vampire's chest. The pointed toe of the heeled boot slammed against it as the assailant yanked his blade back.

"How long have you been hunting in the city of Gilhem, monster?" he asked contemptuously.

The Vampire clutched the slim wound, now gushing silver smoke – trying in vain to seal it – but the blade's magic left it incapable of closing.

"I... I've only been here twice..." the Vampire stammered as he watched the swordsman kneel at his shoulder.

"How many of your kind wear that disguise now?" the man inquired while raising the brim of his hat.

The Vampire noticed the man was not as he imagined. He was not a grizzled fighter with scars covering his cheeks or brow, nor did he have the shadowy stubble his rough voice implied. He had thin pointy features and a smooth face. His clothing consisted of the same billowing sleeves and slim trousers that were popular amongst the Royal youth.

"You're just a boy?" the Vampire coughed out while grasping his sternum.

The man smiled wryly. "I'm twenty-three now, hardly a boy, I'd say. Yet to someone lingering around for centuries like your kind, I guess I'm considered young," Carneth Allard replied, switching to a seated position, "Yet this boy dispatched someone as experienced as yourself."

The Vampire swung his hand wildly at Carneth, but the clawed fingers were smacked away. The once powerful creature was now relegated to weakness from the chest wound.

"I'll offer this deal, monster. If you're willing to slink back to your lair and tell the rest of your kind to remain hidden in their castle and never step foot in Gilhem," Carneth removed a small vial from a pouch on his belt, "I'll heal your wound with a few drops of this."

The Vampire sneered in anger at being commanded by a human. "You heal me... or my family will find you and rip your spine out!" he demanded before enduring another fit of wheezing coughs.

Carneth stood slowly. "Poor decision, monster."

He gracefully spun his sword into an overhand grip and plunged it into the Vampire's forehead. Another stream of silver fog poured from its skull as the skin turned grey, then cracked and petrified. Its whole body turned to stone before the young man's eyes. Carneth wiped his sword on his sleeve before sliding it back into its sheath. He didn't care that the Vampire's blood left a strong stench; he wanted everyone in Gilhem to know he'd waged war with a Snared soul and won.

He stooped down and picked a white ceramic mask off the ground. It had blue and red slashes of paint across slanted cutouts for eye holes. A mess of sharp teeth was carved around the mouth opening and outlined in black.

'They disguised themselves with this,' Carneth mused, *'and somehow, it changed their appearances to that of a ghoul.'*

He tucked it under his arm, deciding to toy with it later. The barn door creaked as he shoved it open. Stepping onto the dirt path outside, he noticed a few people gawking at him from the safety of a porch several yards away. He lifted two fingers to the brim of his hat and saluted them welcomingly. A woman in the group, wearing a long white and blue dress, stepped down from the porch and jogged towards him. Her braid, a mix of brown and white, waved back and forth as she approached. Carneth hopped onto his horse and started trotting slowly away.

"Wait!" she cried, "Those ghouls, how did you slay them?"

He stopped and looked over his shoulder. "They're not ghouls," he said, motioning towards the barn, "See for yourself."

She looked at the open door, staring into the thick curtain of darkness concealing its contents. Her round watery eyes darted back to him, confused and afraid.

"There's nothing in there that can harm you anymore. I used a blade constructed of silver, and its shape," he snatched his rapier from its sheath and held it aloft, "is similar to a stake at the tip."

The thin, brown-haired woman observed his sword, noticing the tip ended in a triangle that jutted out a bit wider than the rest of the blade. As he twisted it, a circle of magic hovered above the guard.

"I thought that magic died?" she gasped.

Carneth shook his head once, slowly, then removed his wide-brim hat and hung it from a rivet on his saddle.

"So much has changed from when my father was here… unless what he claimed was embellished. He was known for his dramatic flair."

"Your father? Was he…"

Carneth nodded. "However, it seems none of his cohorts carry their duties anymore. I've been on these roads a few years now and haven't crossed paths with a single Wayward."

The woman didn't answer him, only mirroring his thoughts with a furrowed brow and heavy eyes.

"I'm guessing you've no idea where I could reach one of them either?" he asked with a sigh.

The woman crossed her arms and bit her lower lip, trying to fend off the cold fog billowing in from the forest beyond Gilhem's edge. "Are you one of them then, a Wayward?"

He turned back to face the forest. "No. I'm afraid I haven't earned a place amongst their ranks. And considering they've all seemingly disappeared, I likely never will."

The woman raised an arm. "Would you like to stay with us for the night? Mister Tarish has a spare room. I can't imagine you'd want to ride through the night in this chill."

Carneth glanced at his palms, still covered with his enemy's blood. His boots were caked in dirt near the sole, and his shirt was covered in rips and tears.

"I appreciate the offer, ma'am. However, I have lodging elsewhere."

Jerking the reigns, he spurred his horse towards the dense woods. Part of him wanted to accept her offer; his aching muscles and heavy lungs begging for reprieve. Yet he couldn't risk leaving the items in his rented room unaccompanied overnight. While he hoped the Innkeeper held an honest establishment – from what he'd seen in the Midland over the last two years – it was better to avoid providing opportunities for any malfeasance.

Sinking into the folds of a lush burgundy chair, Carneth thanked himself for sparing the extra coin on the better room. He swirled a short glass of brandy before downing it in a quick gulp. After setting it on a small wooden end table, he gave a heavy sigh. Letting his arms hang over the sides of his chair, he took a moment, allowing his earlier exploits to sink in. This was the first instance he'd come across of Vampires wearing those oddly painted masks with their shapeshifting capabilities. The idea that a creature with such power wielded even deadlier magic unnerved him.

"How many of them possess those things?" he mused aloud, glancing at the mask resting on a large dresser.

Heaving himself up from the comfort of his chair, he ambled across the room and scooped it up. Turning it over in his hand, he inspected both sides.

'Maybe I'll test you out sometime,' he thought to himself.

After first arriving in his room, he was going to try it on himself. However, a knotting pit of apprehension in his gut convinced him to wait.

'Who knows if it will be welcoming or hostile towards me...' Carneth thought, recalling a run-in with an unfriendly magical trinket he'd taken from a Warlock a few towns before.

A few spots on his hand still stung from when it had burned him after he tried casting a spell from it.

Opening the middle drawer, he set the mask between a black lacquer box with swirling gold lines and a chained amulet. Turning his attention towards the box, he lifted the lid and stared at several keepsakes belonging to his father, Regus Allard.

'I know I promised to return these to your order, father. Yet, the further I venture into the Midland, the more I believe these items will reside in this box forever.'

He exhaled while closing the lid. 'Hopefully, I can find a town with some indication as to where your former friends have gone.'

CHAPTER THREE

DAVION GRACEFULLY landed on the mossy earth surrounding Peregrine's home. He'd traveled to the Witch's cottage routinely since he required her potion to disguise his humanity. Her house rested deeper in the same bog he'd traveled to when his former order chose to infiltrate the Vampires. The lime-green moss and thin vines surrounding her home crawled up its walls and blanketed her roof. Spots of light-brown wood peeked through the dense clumps of glowing greenery swallowing it. Davion approached the brass loop bolted to the front door and wrapped it twice to announce his arrival. As the door slowly opened on its own, he could see her standing at the other end of the small living room, pouring one syrupy maroon liquid into a vial containing a sparkling white one.

He remembered the first time he arrived at her home. Back then, he was looking for answers after his friends were murdered.

'Which one of those bloodsuckers told you to make that potion?!' he'd ordered.

His face flushed with redness and rage, his hands colorless from harshly gripping the sleeves of her billowing dress.

She looked down at his hands with eyes black as a beetle, then returned to meet his furious stare. *'Like Gerine told you all before, it was another of my sisters working in concert with the Royal Court,'* she answered flatly.

Letting go of her sleeves, he was taken aback by her condescending tone. *'Then why would you help us?'*

'Balance,' she replied.

Even though her reason felt shallow, he knew she was being honest. Their place beyond Qulàire's wall was an unintentional equalizer, as Witches and Warlocks shared their work with outsiders in a calculated manner. Many believed they wished to sway the direction of the populations surrounding them.

'They knew Gerine would discover this,' Davion said aloud, *'That bloodsucker hoped we'd strike. Leading us into a cage and closing the door.'*

She waddled over to a table and pulled out a chair for him.

'Sit here, Davion. If you're looking for answers, you can speak with Sister Penelope, although I can't guarantee what she's willing to share.'

Davion had located Sister Penelope and spoken with her all those years ago. He was fortunate that she'd disclosed her buyer, Count Hathric Malnuvious. Of course, Hathric was one of the few Vampires slain that fateful night when the Waywards were discovered hiding amongst the Royals. After the blood-soaked brawl between them concluded, the Vampires held court and laid blame on House Malnuvious. Accusing them of sneaking the Waywards within their ranks to slowly eliminate enemies and eventually take the throne. All within their House were eviscerated for treason. Hearing that name as the only source from Penelope was the first of a trend. Every facet of information he uncovered was fruitless.

'If Hathric had been alive, she wouldn't have told me,' Davion thought when recalling that memory.

Witches and Warlocks shared their recipes but refused to disclose anything regarding who purchased their wares. Which is why aligning with one was so important. It gave you access to incredible magic with complete anonymity.

"Unless they're dead..." Davion muttered, shifting his gaze away from reminiscing and back to Peregrine.

She slid out the same chair for him from all those years ago. "Come have a seat, Davion."

Waddling to her stove, she started boiling water in a turquoise kettle as Davion leaned back in the stiff wooden chair. The interior of her home was not dissimilar from the outside, as trinkets and vials ran up her walls on hooks and shelves in the same manner vines and moss crawled along its exterior. Davion noticed one shelf in particular, which held the golden broach the Waywards once wore. A set of three arrows stretched out in the shape of a *'W,'* with a thin circle behind it. The circle had diagonal lines etched in an even pattern throughout, and on the two sides opposite the arrows were pearlescent beads. Next to the broach was a set of vials and pouches he assumed contained the ingredients for his potion. As he scanned the other shelves, he noticed a large curvy glass with a medallion featuring a Wolven tribe's crest. Or at least he assumed it was one due to its interconnected oval swirls.

"It's ready," Peregrine's raspy voice croaked.

She shuffled over to him with several vials containing the red and black inky substance. Taking them with a thankful grin, he slid them into a leather satchel with multiple miniature pockets.

"Considering the amount I gave you before, Davion, you shouldn't need to dip into that supply for some time."

Davion smiled. "I know. You complain about it every time, Peregrine. I prefer being prepared with plentiful backstock."

She stood in front of him and gently clasped her hands, which barely snuck out the sleeves of her dark green shawl. While she found his requests came far too early, she always acquiesced. His excessive preparedness only surfaced after surviving the slaughter of his companions. The destruction of his world.

He rose from his chair and affixed the satchel to the back of his belt. "One day, I'll convince you to teach me this recipe," he said with a smirk, "Then I won't have to bother you every month."

Peregrine lowered her chin and chuckled. "You don't have the coin to afford excluding that recipe."

He raised an eyebrow. "What do you think I'm saving for while running errands as a messenger for the court."

She casually tapped the table. "I won't believe it until you place the appropriate stack of gold right here."

He returned a quick nod. She was right to be skeptical. It took an incredible sum to exclude a Witch's recipe from being sold openly, with an even higher cost attached if you wished to learn how to brew it. A few floorboards creaked under his heeled boots as he approached her door.

"Peregrine?" he asked, looking back one last time.

"Yes?" she replied quizzically.

"One day, I'll stack that coin on your table, so don't go sharing my secret yet."

She laughed before turning and shuffling back to her stove, waving him off. "You say that every time, Davion."

A tubby hand swiped the dust from a cluttered shelf before snatching a thick tome. Martin Viruticus pulled the pair of thick spectacles from his front vest pocket to better inspect the gold lettering pressed into the blue leather binding.

'Logbook for hired knives. Yes, this one should have the list I need,' he assured himself.

Martin was the recordkeeper for House Viruticus. Usually, his days were spent thumbing through books and sipping cold-pressed blood with one leg crossed over the other. Occasionally he'd have to leave his shelved nest to speak with other House record keepers, then write periodicals updating his leader. Overall, his occupation was one of ease and longevity. Yet today, he'd been tasked with something he hadn't done since the Vampiric Court captured most of the Midland for their secret human farming. Count Geldam Viruticus, leader of his House, ordered him to research any contract killers who wielded a blade that could turn their kind into dust.

'Human farming...' Martin thought with a frown at recalling that phrase.

He preferred the term "blood orchards." It was one shared by many in his field, as they viewed it as more linguistically clever and less garish.

Pressing his glasses close to his nose, he wiped back thin grey strands of greasy hair. *'This book should have it,'* he thought while frantically flipping through the yellowing pages.

It hadn't been opened in ages, nor should anyone need to. The Court had secretly conquered the northern Midland and installed puppet rulers throughout the human settlements. Each Duke presided over land meant to cultivate their subjects as food for the Vampires. The humans were oblivious to their covert rule, and having eliminated the only organized group of protection, mercenary work was a bankrupt venture. Yet the Duke presiding over Gilhem recounted the story of a human wielding a thin blade who turned the Count's son to stone.

Martin absentmindedly licked the tip of one fang, nervously tracing his finger over a written list of cutthroats and their preferred weaponry. Before the Waywards had fallen, the Court had hired human hatchet men to discretely carry out executions from time to time. However, those days were well behind them. The idea seemed implausible to him, but the Count demanded answers, so Martin turned to the only record books containing a possible lead.

'One of them must wield a blade with that power...'

"Did the Count finally put you to work, Martin?" a voice asked from across his desk.

Martin started, his eyes darting away from the pages towards the person who approached him.

"Davion?" he replied quizzically.

"I just got back from visiting Duke Roycen. He wasn't too happy with the news I brought. Still, he signed his approval for the hunting declaration," Davion said, placing an envelope on Martin's counter, "Even though I know those boys wouldn't wait for me to return with this document to begin anyways."

"You need to see Count Viruticus immediately!" Martin blurted out.

He opened the wooden half-door that let him out from behind his enclosed counter and rounded his desk towards Davion.

"What's going on, Martin?" he asked.

He returned Davion's query with an anguished frown. "The Count's son was killed…"

Davion looked over his shoulder quickly before leaning closer. "Is there someone you suspect within the Court?" he asked in a hushed whisper.

Martin looked down while nervously licking the edge of one fang.

"The culprit was human," he eventually croaked.

Davion's stomach twisted anxiously as a chill ran from the back of his ears to the base of his spine. Their own kind covertly offing one another was unexpected but not out of the question, as treachery within the Court was never spoken of aloud but did occur. A human killing them was inconceivable. The Vampires hadn't suffered a casualty from one in almost a decade. Was there a possibility one of the few who broke their bonds and left Moncroix had returned?

No, he couldn't believe that, but he had to know more.

"You're sure of this?" Davion asked, eyes narrowing as he intently stared at Martin.

The record keeper nodded slowly. "I was looking for anyone we've contracted in the past who wields magic this killer used. No one we've hired possesses a sword of that nature."

"What nature?" Davion inquired.

Martin hurried back behind his counter and slid the open book in front of Davion, then pointed at a list of handwritten notes.

"None of the mercenaries we've hired carry a blade that can turn us into ash. And from my notes relating to other Houses, they haven't heard of it either."

Davion raised an eyebrow. "The assailant wielded a sword that burned the Count's son to cinder. Was the blade thin?"

Martin's eyes grew wide with excitement. "Do you know someone not listed here with that power from your time as a Hunter?"

'I've said too much,' Davion cursed to himself. He then quickly covered himself with a simple lie. "I've heard rumors of a Warlock who carried a long metal staff. Many mistook it for a sword."

Martin squinted, internalizing Davion's answer. "It's possible a Warlock was involved, but it seems very unlikely for one to attack us like this. They usually keep to themselves."

Davion rubbed his chin, surveying the record book. "May I borrow this?"

"Of course," Martin answered.

Davion collected the volume under his arm, then strode off. All the while trying to recall which member of his former order sheathed such a sword on their hip.

His heeled boots clicked along the hallway's marble floor as he strode towards the back entrance to the assembly hall of Viruticus Manor. While entering through the main doors would show better decorum, considering the grave nature of recent events, his superior would understand why he took the shorter route from Martin's archives.

The recent news stirred his emotions like a stew made of excitement and dread. Part of him wanted to know everything about this swordsman, believing he might carry a sliver of hope that he could finally free himself. The other half accepted the grim reality that no one was coming to rescue him from this purgatory. Even someone capable of killing his kind.

'No,' Davion reminded himself, *'I'm not one of their kind.'*

He swallowed back the apprehensive lump growing in his throat, bringing his eyes forward. Thin gold trim decorated the white door before him. At the center was a gold knocker shaped like a hippoar's skull. House Viruticus took on the squat, tusked mammal as their symbol. He found it slightly humorous that the Count mirrored the physicality of one, with his plump frame and bulky fangs similar to the beast's shape and teeth.

While they both seemed like jovial creatures, neither could be taken lightly. Similar to the swamp-dwelling hippoar, when Count Geldam's temper flared, he could shred any man – and even some Vampires – into a pile of pulp. Tonight, he would surely be in one of those moods. He looked down with a heavy sigh, then pushed the door open.

The usual five men sat around the long oval table made of black granite with white veining. Highmaster Erickson and his two subordinates – who led the Hunting Division of their House – were still squabbling amongst each other. They probably felt they'd carry the majority of blame from Count Geldam. So, they took turns verbally lobbing that burden back and forth to one another, hoping they wouldn't be the last one left holding it.

Viscount Reginam – second in command of their House – sat to the left of the table and was speaking heatedly in a hushed tone with Baron Taktarov. In the center of it all, with his face half-buried in one hand, sat Count Geldam Viruticus.

Reginam noticed Davion first, turning away from Taktarov, who sat back with his arms crossed, visibly beleaguered from their heated dialogue.

"Martin told me what happened," Davion said quietly, "and I offer my condolences, Count Geldam."

The Count only raised his eyes to meet Davion, head still resting against his pudgy palm. Silence held the room, waiting for their ruler's reaction.

Finally, Geldam broke it. "Considering you only just heard from Martin, I'm assuming you didn't bring any new information with you?"

Davion shook his head. "I'm afraid n..."

He jolted back as Geldam slammed a fist onto the oval table.

"He was going to take my place!" Geldam roared, a crack left on the table beneath his fist, which now trembled with rage.

He steadied himself with a deep breath as everyone in the room reflexively froze. In a show of solidarity, Highmaster Erickson gave Geldam a hefty pat on the shoulder and squeezed. Geldam nodded towards him in gratitude.

"He was the most ferocious Hunter I knew, and he would have served our House well had he taken charge, Sir," Erickson stated. His gravelly voice gave the compliment an added sense of gravitas.

Geldam's lips curled into a snarl. "Something must be done about this."

"We'll find the bastard who committed this terror and bring his head back as a trophy," Erickson reassured him.

Davion pressed his index finger onto the cold table. "Add myself to that roster, Highmaster."

Everyone turned towards him with a perplexed expression. Davion hadn't been a Hunter for several years. He'd stepped down from that role to run letters and petty errands as House Messenger. After hearing a human had slain several Vampires – and Hunters no less – Davion couldn't miss this opportunity.

Count Geldam nodded thankfully. "It would bring me great joy to see you hunt for us again, Davion," he said before turning back to Erickson, "Bring him to me alive. I want to see the look in his eyes when I feast upon his carotid!"

"Of course, Sir," Erickson replied firmly.

Davion leaned forward against the table. "If you'll allow it, Count Geldam, I wish to take my leave now. I'll need time to prepare for such a dangerous excursion," he requested.

Geldam casually waved his bulky hand. "Of course, Davion."

Davion bowed before exiting the room quietly. As he strode down the hallway towards his quarters, his mind centered on one important thought.

'How do I reach this man before they do?'

CHAPTER
FOUR

THE BAR WAS faintly lit by a few candles resting on dusty saucers. Old wood creaked under every booted step of the patrons, who chatted heartily. Most of the men occupying the tavern were tradesmen taking reprieve after making a few coins off their harvested wares. Entertaining themselves in a dismal town that offered little to sustain someone's interests unless they enjoyed cheap liquor.

Yaspen took a sip from a short glass partly filled with a clear liquid. He grimaced after swallowing the moonshine – or at least what this town considered moonshine – then grabbed his utensils and sliced into a leg of lamb. Luckily, they had some decent livestock in the surrounding farms, so he was able to get a decent cut of meat. Yaspen inspected the sliver of lamb on his fork. Unlike the human men in this Tavern, he could actually see quite well. Being a Vampire gave him distinct advantages over an un-Snared soul.

'Extra rare... perfect,' Yaspen thought.

He took the bite and chewed until it was tender, then slid it under his upper lip. After a careful bit of maneuvering with his tongue, he was able to slide the bloodiest bit against the section of gums where one of his fangs once resided. He sighed in relief upon feeling the veins in those stumpy sections soak up some blood. It would pacify his thirst for now.

Lambs were among the few animals whose blood was worth drinking, but it didn't compare to the delicacies prepared during his time in the Royal Court. They really knew how to make a meal out of it. Blood from humans fed on a fruit-heavy diet turned into a rich glaze and drizzled over roasted carrots being one of his favorites. Eyes closed and reminiscing about the recipe, he licked his lips and sucked on another rare piece.

Yaspen opened his eyes.

'Not even close,' he muttered to himself after swallowing.

The majestic events, exquisite attire, and lavish meals were a thing of the past. He'd been convicted of trespassing on another House's grounds. Despite it being a minor crime, his punishment was being defanged and cast off to the northern Midland, one of the regions not secretly under their rule. Most in his position would have tucked tail and wallowed in their loss.

Not Yaspen.

He made the most of his connections and knowledge to embark on a new trade, eventually becoming an extremely successful traveling merchant. So much so that many within the Court purchased from him. In secret, of course.

He looked down at his meal and noticed there were only a few small pieces left. Yaspen gave his surroundings a careful glance to ensure no one was watching. His status as a Vampire – even a defanged one – would be ill-received in this town. Once he felt safe enough, he popped out the sharp claws at the ends of his bony fingers and feverishly shredded the last bits of lamb. After licking his claws clean, he shoved the minced pile of bloody meat under his upper lip, like a man would chew on tobacco.

He stared out the window and watched for anyone riding towards the tavern, hoping to get an early glimpse of the man he was supposed to meet. Rain from the dark sky lightly pecked at the glass, partially obstructing his view. He squinted at the darkness beyond the window but didn't see anyone. He tried to quell his growing impatience by licking the empty spot on his gums again. It was a hard habit to break.

'Maybe one day I'll find a way to replace these,' he mused.

He'd heard rumors from another merchant that people within the Intercontinent of Lor-Rev made mechanical versions of his missing appendage. While that nation used the most advanced technology, it still seemed ridiculous. The merchant in question was also not the most reputable. However, if someone from Lor-Rev heard about the things he'd seen and experienced, they'd likely laugh him off as well. Anyone who visited from another nation within the Intercontinental Forum only saw Qulàire. International travelers weren't allowed past the city's wall. At least not legally, which was why his ability to acquire goods beyond their homeland made Yaspen a very wealthy man.

He sucked a little more juice from the meat resting beneath his upper lip, turning his gaze towards the front door. He'd taken a seat in the furthest corner of this establishment.

Yaspen retrieved a gold pocket watch from the interior of his heavy overcoat.

'He's got one more minute.'

He leaned forward, resting his chin on his hand while absentmindedly rubbing the edge of his mustache with his thumb.

The door swung open, and a man in dark clothing wearing a large brim hat sidled past the crowd and then strode to his table.

Yaspen smiled as he approached. "You're late."

Carneth took a seat on a rickety wooden chair across from him. "My apologies. Venturing here through that weather made my travels quite difficult."

"Your horse can't run in the mud?" Yaspen retorted.

"Apparently," Carneth answered sarcastically.

"One of my messengers said you had an item for me to appraise?" Yaspen asked, rubbing his thumb and forefinger over the muttonchops connected to his mustache.

Carneth nodded and pulled out one of the hunting masks he'd obtained from the Vampires and placed it on the table. Yaspen swallowed his surprise and held his tongue. Like any good salesman, he kept his internal feelings and exterior presentation as separate entities.

"Do you know what this is?" Carneth asked, breaking the silence.

Yaspen played dumb and casually reached for the mask to inspect it. Carneth quickly snatched it from the table, worried the merchant might put it on his face. Assuming Yaspen's cool demeanor meant he was unaware of its power.

"I take it you're not familiar then?" Carneth asked while placing the mask back in his satchel.

Yaspen leaned back and folded his arms. "I was just curious which family House its markings belonged to."

46

Carneth observed Yaspen with a quizzical frown. "Family markings?"

Yaspen chuckled at his ignorance and leaned across the table. "I believe we should continue this conversation somewhere without prying eyes and perked ears."

"I'd rather we continue our conversation here," Carneth objected, resting his hands on the table while interlacing his fingers.

"I'm guessing your time in the Midland hasn't been too favorable. Betrayed a few times, eh?" Yaspen asked while resting an arm on the back of his chair. He pointed at the barkeep, "I'm friends with the owner of this establishment. We can use his stockroom to discuss this further. You can even have your man over there stand outside the door."

Carneth raised an eyebrow. "My man?"

"You think I didn't notice that man in the suspenders and bowler hat over there, watching us out of one eye since you sat here?" Yaspen scoffed.

Carneth smirked. "You live up to your reputation."

"Hopefully, you didn't pay him too much to watch your back. I have no intentions of robbing you, although... that mask is tempting," Yaspen replied while waving the barkeep over.

Leaning with crossed arms against a row of casks, Carneth watched Yaspen methodically inspect the mask. The merchant idly fingered his chin while turning it this way and that, examining the patterns. Finally setting the mask on a crate between the two of them, he ran one hand through his dark, slicked-back hair.

"It's from House Viruticus. They're a bit lower on the political ladder but still quite formidable. Which member did you steal this from?"

Carneth remained silent.

"Don't tell me you killed them?" Yaspen asked gruffly.

Carneth still didn't answer.

Yaspen rubbed his eyes with one hand. "Now I'm making a deal with a murderer…"

"I protected those people," Carneth interjected.

"Not in the eyes of the Court," Yaspen snapped.

Carneth didn't respond this time, staring at the mask instead. He'd heard stories from his father about the Court. Yet he had no inclination of their scope. Gathering together to hunt unwitting humans in these villages. How had no one uncovered this before? If he hadn't already gotten the mask, he assumed Yaspen would've withheld any information.

'He must believe I'm a dead man,' Carneth thought, *'That's why he's unhesitant to share. Just owning it puts an immeasurable target on my head.'*

"Did you have a price in mind?" Yaspen asked.

Carneth looked up from his daydreaming. "If you can tell me where I can find one of the Waywards, it's yours."

Yaspen froze. How long had it been since someone had asked about them? And so blatantly? After their charade using Count Malnuvious' potion, it wasn't more than a few years later that everyone consigned them to memory.

"I'm afraid I can't help you there," Yaspen answered, "The Court finished them off years ago."

Carneth's eyes narrowed. "What do you mean?"

Yaspen glanced at the mask, then back at Carneth.

48

"Fine, the mask is yours," Carneth answered.

Yaspen smiled, snatching it from the crate.

"We have a deal," he said, holding it aloft and tilting it in a makeshift salute, "The men of that order made a very foolish decision. One that took their last breaths," he continued, "They decided to spy inside the Court. Disguising themselves. Of course, they were found... and dealt with," as Yaspen finished, he drew a finger across his throat.

Carneth kept one arm crossed and held his chin, digesting the news.

'Is that why my father left?' he asked himself.

His father never mentioned the details of how or why he'd vacated the order. Considering the passion his father had for being a Wayward, he'd never understood why he left the order.

'He must have disagreed with them on this. Knowing it was a fool's errand, just like Yaspen did,' he rubbed his chin, pondering further, *'But if my father left for that reason, then there must be others who did as well.'*

"Not all of them were slain that night," Carneth said, "You must have heard something about men who abandoned the order before their plan was enacted."

"You make a good point," Yaspen answered, looking away to rack his mind.

After a moment of contemplation, he turned back to Carneth. "I'm afraid I can't think of anyone still on this Intercontinent. I imagine leaving would require them to break their Snare to the Spirits. A trait those men were lucky to have. I've never heard how they did it, but as I'm sure you're aware..."

"They're required to leave Moncroix," Carneth interrupted with a sigh.

Yaspen strode over to a shelf containing several bottles made of dark-brown glass. "I'm sorry I can't be of more help," he said while selecting one, "When the next hunting party comes for you – and it will – maybe they'll have a better answer," as he finished, Yaspen tossed the bottle to Carneth.

Catching it, Carneth looked down at the bottle of alcohol with a beige label covering the front. He then noticed Yaspen walking away.

"How's this supposed to help?" he asked.

Yaspen stopped at the door, turning back to Carneth. "You might as well enjoy the last days you have left."

CHAPTER FIVE

COUNTESS FIONA MAYJERE held the Hunting Mask between her fingers and inspected it. It was the only one left behind after the assailant murdered Geldam's son and his two friends. She pitied Geldam, he was an emotional man who – unlike many of her colleagues – seemed to actually care for those within his House. She couldn't say the same for his son, Thadric. He was spoiled by the opulence bestowed on him and abused every connection he'd obtained.

'That boy almost revealed everything to the humans,' she harshly muttered.

When Duke Roycen had spoken with the townspeople, they claimed to have seen ghouls. However, after the culprit had killed Thadric and his friends, he'd left behind one mask and claimed their predators were really Vampiric in nature. Of course, anyone who witnessed the events was dealt with. Any humans from Gilhem were highly sought after for their blood's hearty flavor. The opportunity to feast on those witnesses was snatched up quickly.

Fiona eventually set the mask down on a small end table next to her chair. She'd been asked to inspect it since her House manufactured them. She'd discovered how to craft them while working with Count Malnuvious during their attempts to improve the potion which masked the Spirit's Snare. The potion became a failure. At least in the practical sense. It did, however, allow her to finally enact her ambition of creating hunting ground villages. Of course, the remainder of the Court was oblivious to her involvement with the potion. She'd ensured her own innocence by letting him take the fall before he could reveal her culpability.

She was a realist and knew what the rest of the Royals refused to admit. Vampires were not ambitious creatures. They only had enough fortitude to develop a comfortable place for themselves. Once entrenched, a Vampire would continue their routine for as long as they lived. At their hearts, they were truly parasites. Fiona accepted this completely without reservations or the gaudy self-judgment many of her peers would undoubtedly express. She knew what her kind really was and planned to accentuate their strengths, so the entire Court could live comfortably.

It led her to set a trap for the Waywards, luring them in with the failed potion as bait. What she hadn't expected was for them to reverse engineer the recipe, allowing themselves to mimic her kind. Fiona had expected them to be more upfront in their response. Luckily, she'd caught wind from an informant about that unexpected hiccup. It was easy then to construct a narrative that Malnuvious yearned for the throne and planned to use infiltrators as a means of snatching it.

After the Court slaughtered them all, she'd convinced the two highest families to begin her plans to control the northern Midland. With the area's only organized protection finally removed, they easily instituted puppet leaders throughout.

'What to make of this situation,' she wondered, *'A man wielding a magical sword is somehow dropped into our kingdom's lap.'*

He couldn't be a Wayward. From her sources, the only remaining ones had fled before their foolish gambit. But he held a sword that was clearly Snared and possessed the skill to defeat three Vampires. Had one of them returned for vengeance?

Rising from her chair, Fiona took the mask with her to a large writing desk on the opposite side of her sitting room. Brushing back her wavy auburn locks for a better view, she placed the mask in the center of it. After retrieving a small perfume bottle from a drawer, she sprayed its misty contents at the mirror, then the mask. The mask shook, then puffed amber smoke from its mouth towards the mirror. While waiting for the mirror to absorb it, she returned the perfume bottle to the drawer. All her potions were in decorative vessels, giving this process the sophistication she believed it deserved.

The glass shimmered so violently that it looked like a writhing corpse. Which wasn't entirely inaccurate. When making the masks for the other Houses, she included ingredients in the recipe, which let her see the last moments of whatever lives it took – and in this rare instance – the final acts of its bearer. The masks had many incredible features woven within. Features she kept secret. If the other Royals knew all their capabilities or could access them, she'd lose substantial political influence.

Peering at the mirror, she waved two fingers in a clockwise circle. Wafts of smoke rushed across the glass, covering the memories of many fallen humans as she passed them toward the final memory.

"There," Fiona whispered.

Thadric was looking at a young man, barely beyond his teenage years. He wore a large brim hat and dark clothing that outlined his figure. He must have been from Qulàire, considering few within the Midland wore such fashionable clothing.

"You lost your life to him?" she laughed.

A knock interrupted her.

"Countess?" a feminine voice called out from behind the door.

"Come in, Adelina," Fiona called back.

Adelina, wearing a blush pink dress, stepped inside and took a seat on a small couch.

"Have you spoken with him?" Fiona asked.

"With whom?" Adelina replied.

Fiona left her desk and took a seat in a chair opposite Adelina. "With Davion. I'm hoping you can bend his ear on what House Malnuvious is planning."

Adelina leaned forward, confused. "Weren't you given the mask? I thought they'd disclose more with you than whatever Davion might know," she leaned back in her seat, "Besides, he's only a messenger now and rarely does anything of consequence."

Fiona rubbed her chin with one finger. "I'm assuming he'll be hunting this culprit down along with everyone else. We'll need to leverage every connection we have, so I can speak with this killer before House Viruticus tears him to shreds."

Adelina crossed her arms. "What are you not telling me, auntie? I thought we weren't getting involved in this?"

Fiona waved off her discouraged stare. "I'm not hiding anything from you. I only chose to get involved once I found out the culprit was human…"

"Human!?" Adelina interjected.

Fiona nodded. "Yes, that's what was reported to me by Duke Roycen when he had Thadric's mask delivered. I'll only get so much time with it before Geldam will demand to have it back."

Adelina leaned forward, pressing a finger onto the oval knee-height table between them. "Shouldn't there be two more masks you can inspect?"

Fiona tilted her head and sighed. "The killer gave this one to the villagers while the other two are missing."

"We're assuming he took them?" Adelina asked rhetorically.

"That's why finding this killer is so important. His magic and skill are indicative of him being a Wayward. If he is one, we need to find him first and discover whatever else he has planned. Imagine if he can utilize the mask to continue hunting our kind."

Adelina nodded. "I'll see what I can uncover, auntie."

Fiona nodded kindly while taking a truffle from a silver plate resting on the table between them.

"Are those cranberry truffles?" Adelina asked enthusiastically, plucking one from the plate.

Fiona finished her bite, savoring the decadent flavor of sour cranberries mixed with blood from corpulent humans. Their heavy fat content gave their sanguine fluid a rich taste that paired extremely well with the tartness of the berries.

"If he's tight-lipped about their plans, I'll need you to shadow him," Fiona said, watching Adelina enjoy her truffle.

Adelina closed her eyes and licked the remaining blood-infused chocolate from her fangs.

Finished savoring the morsel, she looked at her aunt. "Of course," she answered, rising from her seat.

Striding gracefully towards the door, she stopped short of leaving and looked over her shoulder at Fiona. "He'll be needing comfort during such a tumultuous ordeal; I'm sure he'll tell me everything."

CHAPTER SIX

TIGHTENING HIS FOREARM brace, Davion readied his thoughts for combat. It had been years since he'd been in a real fight. Now he was going to try and trace the steps of someone capable of killing three Vampires.

He sat atop his horse and squinted through the pattering rain. He'd taken one of the living horses – rather than the disgusting undead ones – to avoid suspicion. While some Vampires rode the heinous beast wherever they went, Davion relished the chance to grasp any semblance of his former humanity. A normal horse wasn't tireless like the ones reconstructed as horsliches, so it took him most of the night to reach the town of Hailyce.

He'd requested an opportunity to do some reconnaissance before the actual hunt, claiming it would be the safest approach. Considering what had occurred, some of House Malnuvious believed there was more than one person involved. None of the townspeople corroborated that notion. Yet, the possibility existed, creating the fear of one lone swordsman, so keeping more in secret reserve made sense.

'It would be a smart tactical move,' Davion told himself.

After the incident at Gilhem, the swordsman rode southwest. Davion planned to pursue that route, visiting late-night establishments of nearby villages in hopes of discovering his whereabouts.

'I only have a few days before the Count will send everyone,' he thought.

Dismounting, Davion's boots sunk into the muddy earth. He trudged through the muck and rain towards the tavern, holding his hood overhead. His Vampiric skin loved the cold, as their bodies aged incredibly slowly. Touching one felt as though you were caressing a slab of granite during winter. The rain, however, was not comforting. It didn't pour off their skin the same way as humans. Rather, it clung to them like water does to hair.

Finally reaching the small metal awning over the door, Davion wiped the rain from his face and stepped inside.

Warmth.

He felt the raging flames of a nearby fireplace. While various rooms within their castles had fireplaces, they were never installed in such small quarters. He winced at the heat but held his tongue.

He had to blend in.

Immediately after finding a seat, he was approached by a raven-haired woman wearing a simple brown dress that fell to her ankles.

"What will you have, sir?" she asked him.

"Do you serve any rum?" he replied.

She smiled and nodded affirmingly. As she turned towards the bar to retrieve his drink, he lightly grabbed her wrist, causing her to look back toward him.

59

"Could you pour it over ice?" he requested.

The woman smirked and raised an eyebrow, intrigued by his ask. Davion released his touch, but she didn't pull away. After a moment of hesitation, she finally took her gaze from him and brushed her dark bangs across her forehead.

"Yes, I'll make sure it's poured over ice for you, Sir."

Davion leaned back in his seat and watched her make her way across the room. He let out a deep sigh. He felt everything, her steady pulse, her lavender perfume, the sweet peppery scent made by the faint amount of sweat in her hair. Although their sense of smell was weak, a Vampire's touch absorbed a larger array of sensory input from a human than just the nature of their skin.

He exhaled slowly, calming his nerves.

Touching her was risky. His hunger hadn't been satiated by a live human in some time. It was hard to let someone with such ripe blood walk away. Her figure and smile didn't make that choice any easier, either.

He needed to stuff his bloodthirst away. She had to stare into his violet eyes willingly. His trance would only be effective if she welcomed his visual advance. It didn't allow him any real control over her. It just left her susceptible to his advances. Creating a desire to be near him. It was the oldest way of hunting humans. Throughout history, men had completely miscategorized the power, embellishing the nature of it and assuming one could control your every waking thought if you stared into their eyes for a prolonged period.

"Here's your rum," she said, gracefully setting a small glass at his table.

He quickly took a sip, hoping to take the edge off his thirst.

"Miss, I hate to be so forward, but when are you done tending to the whims of these patrons?" he asked, setting the glass down.

The woman blushed. "Well, our family runs this tavern, so I'm here quite late…"

Davion nodded towards a stout, bearded man passing a mug across the counter to another customer. "Is that your father behind the bar?"

"Yes," she replied.

Davion quickly downed the rest of his drink.

"Tell your father he pours an incredible rum, and I'll need another round," he said while handing the glass to her.

She took the glass eagerly and went to retrieve another. Davion turned in his seat to observe the other patrons, looking for a young man of tan skin and Qulàire garb. No one inside matched the description they'd been given from Duke Roycen.

'Maybe he's changed his appearance to hide from retaliation?' Davion wondered.

He then looked for anyone with a thin rapier on his belt, yet found no swordsman openly carrying it. His browsing was interrupted as another drink was set before him. Without looking at the young waitress, he downed the shot in one sip and set it at the edge of the table.

"Here's the coin for this, Miss. You can keep any extra for yourself." Davion placed four coins next to the glass. "I'll be taking my leave. Thank you for the remarkable rum," he finished, rising from his seat.

He felt the rhythmic thumping of a youthful pulse in his ears. The waitress grabbed his hand.

"Don't go…" she asked.

Davion looked at her over his shoulder.

"Well, at least not that way. If you come through the back, you won't need to walk around the building to get to the horse stall. I'm assuming you rode here?" she continued.

He nodded, then gestured for her to lead the way. She took him past a few small tables to a door at one side of the bar. Her father turned from cleaning a mug to give the pair a quizzical glance as they passed him.

Outside, the rain still fell but quietly, a mere drizzle. This was the second town he'd visited, and still hadn't noticed anyone matching the young assailant. Unfortunately for this woman and her father, he'd have to change course. He needed to leave some breadcrumbs in hopes his target would stumble upon them and take a bite.

"Thank you for the shortcut. I'll make sure to stop here again," he said, turning to face her.

"Please, stay a bit longer," she begged.

Davion stepped forward and slid his hand behind her head, running his fingers through her wavy hair. Grasping it tightly, he twisted her face and kissed her neck. He curled his upper lip and pressed one fang to the skin covering her carotid. One pinprick was all he could allow for the moment; he couldn't feast upon her yet. One jagged tooth sucked the droplet that dribbled out. A sensation of hot needles raced down his spine at the taste of her fresh, youthful blood.

"What are you doing with my daughter!" a voice bellowed.

It was the woman's father.

'Finally,' Davion thought, sighing with relief.

She was merely bait.

He tossed the girl aside and turned to run. The barkeep charged after him, grabbing the back of his shirt before he could flee. He yanked Davion backward and sent him tumbling across the mud. Davion stuck out a hand to stop himself. He reached into his coat, retrieving his hunting mask. His head bowed, hair covering his face, he slid the mask on without anyone noticing.

"Did you think you could slink in here and…"

The barkeep froze in place as he watched Davion - or at least what once was Davion – rise from the ground.

"Y-you're a ghoul?!" the barkeep stammered in horror.

To him, Davion appeared as a veiny muscled gargoyle.

"Father!" the woman screamed.

"Run inside, dau…"

Davion rammed one clawed finger into the man's stomach, making sure to avoid any vital organs. Blood seeped from the wound around his finger as he turned and hissed at the young woman. She saw spittle fly from a jagged range of yellow teeth, only witnessing the mask's display of his movements and not his true form. Davion let go of the man's stomach, letting him slump to the muck. Groaning in agony, the barkeep clutched at the puncture in his belly as Davion darted toward the woods.

He heard loud clamoring inside the bar behind him as he whistled for his horse to meet him. Before enough of the patrons could rally and possibly thwart his assault, he was mounting his ride several yards into the woods and charging away. Despite the brutality of his work tonight, everything was carefully controlled.

Word would spread of the scene and hopefully reach the ears of the man he sought after.

CHAPTER
SEVEN

CARNETH LISTENED TO the woman's story intently.

"You're saying a man sought your attention, and when your father confronted him, he morphed into a ghoul?" Carneth inquired once she was finished.

Her thick black hair fell over her face as she looked to the floor and nodded affirmingly. Carneth rose from his barstool and set a coin on the counter. Giving a nod to the barkeep before walking away from the dark-haired beauty.

Her gaze shot towards him in shock as he abruptly left. She'd heard this man had slain several ghouls one town over in Gilhem, saving an entire family. She didn't expect him to desert her after hearing their plight.

He stopped just before the door, barely turning his head to observe her from the corner of his eye. She took the hint and eagerly followed him outside.

"Why speak with me here?" she asked, clutching her arms around herself. Staving off the chilling evening wind as best she could.

"Too many perked ears within that tavern. Now that you've given everyone inside an idea of who I am, I need to find a new place to rest my head, lest I lose it while I sleep," Carneth replied calmly.

The woman frowned. "Why would any of them harm you? You'd be saving us."

Carneth scanned the area before he answered. From what he could see, they were alone.

"If that ghoul was once a man, what's to say there aren't more of them hiding amongst you?" he asked.

She answered with affirming silence.

He took them down a cobblestone alleyway between two closed stores. Remembering another Inn was nearby, he wanted to reach it before they closed their doors for the evening.

The wooden stairs creaked under Carneth's heeled boots. Passing a small window, he could see the sun was only a sliver away from descending completely below the horizon. Behind him, he heard matching creaks as the woman – who said her name was Ophelia – followed. The fact that she so easily trusted him showed either her naiveté or desperation.

"Close the door behind you," Carneth said while removing his jacket.

Ophelia pushed the door until it was within an inch of closing.

He noticed her choice and smirked. "I see you're learning."

Ophelia's expression soured; she didn't find Carneth's observation as amusing as he did.

"Will you help us fight it?" she tersely responded.

Carneth nodded. "I can help you should it return. However, I believe there's something you're not telling me," he said, grabbing a stool and dragging it to the center of the room. Ophelia still stood inches from the door.

Taking a seat, he leaned forward, placing his forearms on his knees. "I'm curious why you think it would come back after clearly showing fear of fighting more than one man."

Ophelia swallowed the lump in her throat and sighed. She reached into a small pocket stitched on the front of her brown dress and retrieved a scrap of paper. Approaching him, she placed it on the little circular table next to his chair, then quickly turned away. His eyes narrowed, intrigued by her clear sign of disgust at whatever it said.

Opening it, he read the scrawled black ink:

I'm not finished.

"Am I supposed to believe this was from a ghoul?" Carneth asked incredulously.

Ophelia faced him and shook her head in frustration. "I found that in my pocket afterwards. I don't understand..."

Unable to say more, she placed a hand over her eyes in an attempt to steady herself. Carneth remained silent, giving her a moment to breathe.

She sighed and dabbed underneath her eyes with a shaky finger. "I believe that creature was toying with us, but I'm not sure why?"

Carneth leaned back in his seat, crossing his arms. "Who told you I could help?"

She turned towards him. "A young boy from Gilhem came to my town with a gift from their farm. They told my family they were saved from three ghouls by a young man with silver and black hair, who wore a pin on his chest just like yours," as she finished, she pointed to the Wayward symbol pinned to his chest.

'An old habit I'll need to break,' he decided, placing a hand on his badge, *'I'll have to tuck you away until I can rid myself of any pursuers.'*

Carneth swallowed uneasily while remembering his fight with the three Vampires. While he believed Ophelia's story, he had to press her to ensure it was genuine. This supposed ghoul that morphed from a human was likely another Vampire.

'Why leave a note like this?' he asked himself, *'Is this one of the men Yaspen spoke of who'd come looking for me?'*

He stood from his chair and tucked the note into his pocket. "Tell me, Ophelia, when was the last time you saw a Vampire?"

She scoffed in confusion. "I know what I saw, and that creature was definitely a ghoul."

He crossed his arms. "I know that. Just answer my question."

She shrugged. "No one has seen any of them since the large cities in the Midland banded together and appointed Dukes. They were able to seal a treaty for our safety from the Vampiric Court and the Wolven tribes. The Gods know we face enough menace from the other creatures lurking in the uncivilized swamps and dark forests surrounding us."

He paused, digesting her words before speaking.

"What if I told you the family I saved was attacked by Vampires who decided to break this supposed treaty."

"Here's a little incentive to spread word of my next arrival," Davion said while dropping a small coin purse into Yaspen's hand.

Yaspen bit the corner of his lower lip while digging a bony finger inside the pouch.

"I can spread the word to the silver savior," he replied after counting his cut.

"Silver savior?" Davion asked, raising one eyebrow.

Yaspen gave him a knowing grin. "The one you seek has garnered quite the reputation. People of the Midland are talking about a young demon slayer with silver streaks through his hair, wielding a magical sword. Some believe he's been sent by the old magic itself."

The old magic,' Davion thought, *'That's what people inside the Duke-led fiefdoms call the Snare.'*

The Court had kept the ability to obtain a Snare hidden from Humans. The only times they ever saw it was stumbling across Warlocks or Witches who lived in Midland towns outside the ones secretly governed by the Vampires. And fortunately for the Court, Witches and Warlocks were just as secretive about how to obtain one.

"From what I've heard, he has this odd habit of asking them about the Waywards," Yaspen continued.

Davion's eyes darted toward Yaspen. It took immense restraint to swallow back the hundred questions that leaped into his throat.

"Even had the pin on his chest," Yaspen continued, leaning one arm against a nearby windowsill and pointing to his chest with the other. He shook his head, "He isn't one of them, though. I believe he's wearing it as a calling card since he's trying to track one down."

"Well, he won't find any," Davion answered calmly, "We finished them off years ago."

Yaspen nodded in agreement. "I told him as much."

"You've spoken with him directly?!" Davion blurted out.

Yaspen took off his hat and placed it on the table between them. He grabbed his drink and took a long swig, making his guest wait several excruciating seconds before answering.

'Ensuring control of the conversation as always,' Davion muttered under his breath.

"He'd been asking around about purchasing certain potions. He knew more about Moncroix magic than anyone I've met from Qulàire."

"Tell me everything spoken between you," Davion said in a calm yet commanding tone.

Yaspen leaned back in his chair and took another sip from his short rum glass. He set the drink down, still holding his tongue.

"Fine," Davion replied, rolling his eyes.

He fished into a small satchel tied to his belt and retrieved another coin pouch. tossing it towards the merchant. It hit the table with a chunky clink.

Yaspen took another sip and then cleared his throat. "As I was saying before, he was very interested in finding a member of that old order. I informed him they were all gone, deserters. When I had no answer for him, he pressed me about the Vampire's hunting habits since he discovered that some of the ghouls he'd slain were actually our kind," finishing his story, he downed the rest of his rum and then stood from his chair.

Davion absentmindedly toyed with a buckle on the leather bracer around his forearm, pondering Yaspen's retelling.

"Did he say how he knows so much about the Midland's history?" Davion inquired.

Yaspen shook his head, "I'm afraid not."

"Do you know where he is now?" Davion asked.

"I don't know that either. Although, I did meet him at a tavern near this outpost. So, I doubt he's far from here," Yaspen answered.

"Send word to your men that you have a lead on the location of a Wayward. I'm sure he'd be willing to speak with you again if he heard that from one of your messengers," Davion said.

"I'm afraid that won't work," Yaspen replied, placing his hat atop his head, "He's too perceptive to believe such a quick turn of valuable information isn't a trap. Especially knowing he's killed several of your fellow Royals," finishing his explanation, he adjusted his hat just so. "Besides, Davion, once I send word about your savagery, I'm sure he'll come looking for you anyways. He seems to enjoy helping humans."

Davion held out an arm, blocking Yaspen's path. "If you won't claim to have the information yourself, then tell him I know where he can find one."

Yaspen looked down at Davion's hand, then back to his eyes. "Alright, but I wouldn't wait for me if I were you. A mysterious man with ties to the Midland's past comes strolling in, murdering Vampires with a Snared sword..." Yaspen's eyes narrowed, "I doubt you'll be the only one looking to question him."

Davion continued to block Yaspen's way, causing him to sigh in frustration.

"What?" Yaspen grumbled.

"If you knew of his transgressions against the Court, why did you let him leave? I'd expect you to bring him to us?" Davion asked.

"Because I'm not part of your Court," Yaspen replied angrily, baring his upper teeth.

Davion held his tongue upon recognizing the two holes where fangs once resided.

Yaspen continued. "He also met me in a public Tavern and hired someone to watch the door, ensuring he made it out safely. If I were caught stealing him away – gagged and bound on my horse – it would destroy my reputation," he pressed a pointed finger into Davion's chest, "And we both know how valuable it is for me to have my ear to the ground with the humans."

He placed a hand on Davion's arm and gently moved it aside. "Don't fret. You'll find him eventually. No one has outrun you during your tenure as a Hunter. It's honestly good to see you back where you belong."

Yaspen tipped his hat in salute to Davion, then briskly left the front lobby, heading upstairs. A few seconds later, Yaspen heard the door close behind him as Davion left his outpost. Of course, he hadn't been entirely truthful with Davion. He did know where the assailant was, as one of his subordinates had seen him meeting a woman at a bar one town over.

'I can't let you find him so easily,' Yaspen smugly thought to himself. 'I want to ensure he has enough time to prepare before you strike.'

He ran his tongue over one of the holes in his gums. After everything the Court had done to him, he felt it was best if a bit more chaos befell their perfect little kingdom.

CHAPTER EIGHT

EVENING RAIN, DRIVEN by the wind, attacked the window ravenously. Carneth wiped the dust from a small pane of glass with a gloved hand and stared outward. He could see the last few people outside, tucked underneath scarves or hoods, scurrying back to their homes. Trying to avoid slipping on the wet cobblestone.

'Hopefully, he takes the bait tonight,' Carneth thought.

He'd asked the young woman, Ophelia, to wander around the streets alone. Hoping she would lure the Vampire out. Of course, she was still convinced the monster was something else entirely. He couldn't disagree. He'd seen many strange things during his travels across the Midland, especially with some of the Warlocks who claimed to provide protection. Although he'd never seen one of them prey on vulnerable people at a tavern like that.

His meeting with Yaspen also left him uneasy. The tradesman had divulged such important information. Information he doubted anyone else had.

'Either that mask was worth more than I realized, or he really does believe I'm a walking corpse.'

Then a third thought crossed his mind.

'Maybe he wants me to eliminate someone for him.'

It wouldn't be the first time someone tried parlaying him against their enemies. A person like Yaspen didn't become the preeminent connection for underground trade without having a few snakes hissing at his heels.

"Should I go out there now?" Ophelia asked.

Carneth – concentration broken – turned from the window to face her. She had an indigo shawl draped over her shoulders, with a dark scarf wrapped around her head to keep the rain off. Tonight, she donned trousers rather than the ankle-length dresses young women often wore.

Carneth nodded. "You'll be the only one out in this weather. Make sure you don't deviate from the path we planned earlier. It's the only course that allows me to trail you while avoiding watchful eyes."

Ophelia nodded in return, acknowledging his directions, then left the room. Carneth observed his sword, left in its sheath on a round wooden table. Through flickering light atop a candle wick, he saw the Wayward symbol carved into the hilt. Despite his qualms about helping Ophelia, something urged him to pull on this thread. To tug the loose string in hopes it would yank free answers he needed.

'Even if I'm being led into a trap by Yaspen, I must see this through. I'll find the answers to give you a proper burial, father.'

Davion knelt at the edge of a small balcony. It was attached to the roof of an animal feed store, with only a modest wall surrounding it. He pressed his shoulder against it, peaking over the side of the railing.

'Do they really think I'm that stupid?' Davion asked himself.

The girl he'd terrorized before was wandering around the night rain. She'd already made one complete pass of the main town road and seemed to be taking the same steps again.

'The townspeople must have set this trap,' he thought, shaking his head, *'I can't imagine someone capable of slaying Vampires being this predictable,'* he tightened the straps on his forearm bracers while pondering further, *'Unless he just got lucky the first time. Those boys were careless and entitled. They brushed off many opportunities to train with me or anyone else who offered. Relying on the Snare's power and nothing more.'*

He quickly traced a finger over a few of his tools, ensuring everything was in place. Dagger in his boot, smoke powder in his front pouch, double-sided axe strapped to his back, hunting mask on his hip.

Davion slowly rose to his feet, then placed one dark leather boot on top of the balcony wall. His black cloak with violet inner lining waved gently behind him. The rain was heavy, but the wind was light. Perfect weather. He pulled free the strand of leather that held his hair in a bun. Thick black locks fell to his shoulders as Davion casually rolled his head, cracking the vertebrae in his neck. Looking at his hands, he tensed his fingers. Talon-like claws shot from their tips. Rain poured over him, droplets sliding off his cloak and deep-green leather armor. The

76

lighter weight and tight fit of his garb suited him better for fighting someone wielding a nimble rapier.

He leaped from the roof towards the girl, hoping he'd lured the right man into this fight. Like a hawk swooping down to steal its prey, he snatched her arm before she saw him coming. Penultimate fear gripped her as she pathetically tried to yank her arm free from his grasp. He stared at her, unmasked, believing his only chance to lure his prey was to avoid a monstrous appearance. She looked up at his violet eyes, her expression beyond fright. The stare of a wounded lamb, knowing the predator intended to spill its last ounce of blood.

"You coward!" a voice cried from another small balcony.

Turning his head, his enhanced vision caught a slender silhouette standing stoically on the balcony. In a single swift movement, he leaped across the street towards the figure, landing in front of him. He snatched the man by the throat.

"Please…" the man stammered.

He was elderly, wearing thin and tapered clothing. Slim trousers, a white cotton shirt, and a snug black vest with gold buttons.

'A trick?' Davion thought.

Sensing something, he ducked, barely dodging an arrow that whizzed past his ear. Releasing his grip, he let the old man fall to his knees, clutching his throat and gagging. Davion turned to see another slim figure – again, in expensive garb – step out from the shadows of an awning across the brick-laid street. He wore a large black hat and ankle-length duster jacket.

"Since that missed, I'll use what worked last time," the man said, tossing his bow aside and unsheathing a thin sword.

Eyes wide, Davion charged off the balcony, lunging towards him. As he flew across the rainy sky, his Vampiric nature made him appear like a blurred mixture of smoke and violet ink.

Hand outstretched, talons one inch from the man's nose, something slammed into Davion's side. He flew sideways through the rain before skidding across the ground. Digging his claws into the stone roadway, he stopped his tumbling and swept himself upright. Furiously wiping the hair from his eyes, he faced his adversary.

A young man stood confidently with his hand outstretched towards the individual Davion had initially lunged for. "Thank you, sir, you're excused. And I'll be needing my sword," Carneth finished while receiving his sword from the man.

Davion tried to attack once more, but the stinging, fiery pain in his side brought him up short. He fell to one knee, clutching his waist.

'A broken rib... how?' he thought frantically, looking at the young man who stalked towards him.

Carneth smiled while noticing the creature's fear and disbelief. "Silver is a weakness for the Snared, no?" he said, rolling his arm in an elaborate stretch.

Through the lamppost light, Davion noticed some form of plating bulging underneath Carneth's sleeve. Davion grimaced through his pain and dashed away, heading towards a poorly lit section of the street.

"Don't be shy, monster," Carneth chided, "Revel in the knowledge your kind is finally entering a fair contest."

He finished his insult with a few intricate slashes, demonstrating his skill. Davion's eyes narrowed, scowling at the

78

swordsman's arrogance. He slowly crept backward, slinking deeper into the darkness. As he retreated to more favorable ground, the remaining townspeople who had assisted Carneth ran for the nearest door, looking to escape the upcoming fight.

Carneth stabbed his sword overhead, and lime-green lines swirled around its hilt. Suddenly, orange fire erupted from the thin blade and surrounded it. He lowered the sword, pointing it at Davion. "If you think cowering in the dark will save you, I'd suggest another tactic." Flames dripped from the sword as he spoke, hissing as they slapped the rain-soaked stone beneath his feet.

Davion watched Carneth carelessly advance on his position. He dug his heels in and readied himself to retaliate, then thought better of it. *'If I fight him here, I can't confront him about what Yaspen said. I need him to think I'm vulnerable and chase me somewhere that I can speak more freely. Somewhere without prying ears.'*

Snatching a small throwing knife from his belt, he haphazardly tossed it at Carneth, who immediately smacked the blade away with his flame-drenched sword. Davion feigned frustration, shrieking and wildly running at Carneth, who sidestepped him and sent a plated shoulder shove into his side. Davion tumbled clumsily across the ground, then scrambled to his feet. Grabbing a wooden fence beam to steady himself, he stuck out his hand for his aggressor to halt.

Carneth stopped just a few feet from him. "Why should I pity you, animal?"

Davion leaned forward. "I know you seek the Waywards," he hissed.

Before Carneth could ingest the words, Davion shot away in a flash of velvet smoke. Carneth stood dumbfounded for a beat, then shook himself free of the stupor and swallowed back his shock. He raced after Davion's clouded figure, leaving behind the lamplight for the complete blackness of the forest ahead.

"Victor!" he yelled before whistling at his horse, who he'd strategically left untethered. Hearing its name and being signaled, his charger galloped after him. Carneth snatched the reins and swung himself onto Victor's back; then, the two raced after the fleeing Vampire.

Davion stood in the upper branches of a tall fir tree, silently waiting for his pursuer to arrive. Several yards away, light – white as a sheet – glowed through the forest. The "silver savior," as he was dubbed by the people, sat atop his horse and trotted carefully along a worn dirt path. Davion watched curiously as Carneth canted his sword and panned it over nearby trunks, inspecting them. The light uncovered violet lines laced with dashes of red.

'He can track traces of someone's Snare?' Davion thought, incredulity mixing with alarm.

He'd seen magic like this from members of his former order, but it was extremely rare to find now. It took a lot of convincing for the right Witch or Warlock to teach you such an important spell. Davion wondered how this young man, who only recently reached notoriety, was able to purchase or steal this hallowed magic.

Carneth yanked his reins, stopping his horse a stone's throw from Davion's perch. "I know you lurk atop these trees, monster. Reveal yourself and explain why you belched those words about the Waywards before you fled."

Davion fluttered to the ground, appearing as a downward swirl of corpulent fog. The smoke curled away, and he stood still, staring down Carneth. "I ask the same of you?"

The two harshly observed each other in dead silence. Both men were battle-tested, and neither seemed willing to give a premature edge.

Carneth begrudgingly broke the impasse. "I'll start by asking if the name, Yaspen, has any meaning to you?"

Davion crossed his arms and smiled. "I'm curious how much he divulged to you about our kind?"

Carneth hardened his gaze and chose his words carefully, not wanting to betray the man who'd given him the only solid lead so far. "I'm sure he divulged my intentions in equal measure, considering you knew to mention my father's order."

A chill ran through Davion, like a frigid knife slicing its point down his back.

"Who was he?" Davion asked.

Carneth frowned impatiently. "Why would you care? So you can tell me whether you dressed his throat with your wretched fangs? I'll have you know he left this Intercontinent before you had the chance to slaughter him."

Davion didn't reply, instead flipping his cloak and leaping up into a set of hefty branches. He steadied himself before letting out a scream at a decibel only others of his kind would hear. Taking a moment, he thankfully received no reply to his hunting call. Stepping off the branch, he dropped to the ground, landing gracefully on his feet. Carneth surveyed Davion, an uneasy expression crossing his face. Davion could tell the young man was lost as to what his intentions were.

"I promise you'll thank me for that," Davion replied coolly.

He studied Carneth's face, trying to place which Wayward he resembled. Luckily, he'd mentioned being the son of someone who'd voted to leave their order. That shortened the list dramatically. Was it Luke... or Harald maybe? No, this man's white hair with streaks of black didn't resemble either of them. Nor did his pointed features.

"Care to explain?" Carneth asked.

"I'm the only Vampire you'll be dealing with in this forest tonight," Davion answered, unfurling one side of his cloak.

Carneth instinctively whirled his sword into a ready position, assuming Davion's gesture was towards his weapon.

Davion slowly raised a palm to calm Carneth. "I'm only resetting my cloak. I don't plan to attack you, so long as you respond in kind."

Carneth's eyes narrowed, glaring at Davion while refusing to sheath his sword. "Enough with the posturing. Tell me what you know about the Waywards because if you simply spewed their name to buy yourself time, I'll carve their insignia across your forehead."

Davion smiled wryly, chuckling and shaking his head. "I appreciate your vigor, boy, but I doubt that sword will touch my flesh."

"Care to test me?" Carneth asked, angling his shoulders and bringing his sword to the ready.

Davion waved him off. "I brought you here to talk. I need to know what you've learned from Yaspen. The Court in Vèspige placed a target on your back larger than your horse, but I've been given first right to hunt, so use this time wisely."

"Hunt or talk, which is it?" Carneth asked with a frown, settling deeper into his fighting stance.

Davion sighed before returning a knowing stare. "I'm the one chan..."

Carneth lunged forward, jabbing at him. Davion leaped back, but Carneth gave him no reprieve, whirling his blade in continuous arcing slashes. Davion, back against a tree, dipped to his side and dodged a thrust that stabbed through the trunk. He looked over his shoulder and noticed wood beginning to rot around the blade.

'Whose blade had that trait?' Davion wondered.

He couldn't remember one of his former companions having so many properties within one weapon. His thoughts were snatched away as Carneth charged him again. Davion took one clawed hand and slashed a nearby tree, spraying husks of bark at his pursuer. Carneth dodged the distraction and then tossed a clump of powder. Davion swung his cloak in front of himself to block whatever substance was hurled in his direction. He watched in surprise as some of the cloth began to smolder.

'Silver powder,' he noted, *'How does he have the coin to afford that?'*

Davion lept skyward and reached into his pouch, snatching a smoke powder. Reaching the apex of his jump, he twisted mid-air to throw it, but his opponent was gone. Using the gliding properties of his Vampiric nature, he threw himself sideways, changing his direction and landing on a tree branch.

83

Higher ground would hopefully uncover Carneth's location and keep him safe from any additional silver weaponry. After hurriedly scanning the area, he still couldn't find him. Only his horse could be seen, standing behind a tree, blowing nervously through distended nostrils.

Davion grimaced in frustration and leaped down. He stood in the middle of the clearing with his arms outstretched, turning in a circle. "I thought you wanted a fight. One display of power, and you run?"

No answer came.

'Who fought with such trickery?' Davion wondered. Still trying to remember who the man's father was.

His sharp Vampiric hearing caught a faint rustling behind him. He unsheathed the axe from his back and spun on his heel, swinging it in an arc. The hefty blade cleaved a silver arrow in two. Davion completed a few tight circular swings with his chosen weapon, displaying his prowess.

"I'd refrain from wasting any more silver. I can't imagine Yaspen set a forgiving price."

Davion heard a pebble roll and turned to find Carneth at his back. He swung his double-sided axe upward with one arm – knocking Carneth's sword away – then stepped through the blow and reached for his opponent's neck. Carneth dipped aside and kicked the back of Davion's heel, causing him to fall. He caught himself and rolled away to avoid any further strikes.

'He wants me to think he's vulnerable. Every attack is meant to lure me in. Who fought with such strong counters?'

Davion continued running through the names of his former colleagues while Carneth inched forward, sword pointed at his chest. Davion heaved his axe overhead and stepped

84

forward, chopping down with all his strength. Carneth lept back as the axeblade slammed into the dirt. The force of the blow cracked the ground a yard in front of Davion. Carneth's foot caught in the crack, tripping him. Davion stuck his foot out and pushed off his axe handle towards him, extended claws ready to slash. Carneth, fallen to one side, kicked a foot into Davion's knee and snatched his wrists, then flung him overhead. Davion twisted his body mid-air, landing on his feet with ease. Carneth scrambled to his sword and took a guarded stance, facing his attacker.

"Regus..." Davion said, whipping his cloak behind him.

Carneth froze in place.

"That's one of Regus' favorite defensive maneuvers. It took me a while to finally place your fighting style, but that right there settled any debate," Davion concluded, walking back to his axe.

Carneth lowered his sword and stood dumbfounded.

"Did your father send you to discover what became of them?" Davion asked while retrieving his weapon and sheathing it behind his back.

Carneth looked away from him. "My father is gone."

Davion sighed deeply. "I'm sorry."

Carneth's face hardened as he stared him down. "Spare me your pity. Yaspen told me the Vampiric Court destroyed every Wayward who stayed behind."

Davion didn't answer.

Receiving no response, Carneth continued. "I came here in hopes of finding one of them. Having learned of their failed plan, I now seek the location of the others who left this Intercontinent."

85

Davion's eyes narrowed. "And what then?"

"I planned to give him a proper Wayward burial," Carneth replied, finally sheathing his sword.

The adrenaline and focus of combat having worn off, Davion felt the emotion of the moment finally reach him. The excited anxiousness of encountering someone who understood the legacy of the Waywards.

Was this his chance to leave? A sign from the Gods, lending their hand to help him escape the prison of living with the Court in Vèspige? Then another thought emerged. Could he really escape his current fate? He'd given up leaving years ago. Resigning himself to impersonate a Vampire for the rest of his days.

'This is what you wanted,' Davion told himself, *'You tracked him down at the mere possibility he knew the Waywards. Now it turns out he's the descendant of one, and you're thinking of hiding again.'*

Of course, it was easy to revel in the realization that he'd finally achieved his objective. Yet, confronted with the reality that accomplishing his goal would leave him a hunted man, it lost all celebratory triumph. He had a decision to make. Reveal himself or slink back to the ease of complacent damnation.

Davion unhooked a pouch and retrieved a small gold emblem from inside, then held it up for Carneth to see.

"I can help you properly bury your father," Davion stated, proudly displaying his Wayward badge.

CHAPTER
NINE

COUNT GELDAM VIRUTICUS rapped his fingers anxiously on the table. Davion had left for his reconnaissance days ago, and he hadn't received word of his whereabouts.

"I figured he'd have sent a courier bat by now?" Geldam complained.

Grabbing his goblet with a shaky hand, Geldam took a significant swig, dribbling a little blood wine on his chin. Rather than reach for the napkin, he swiped the red remnants with his palm.

"I need another drink," Geldam grumbled before taking another sip, this time savoring it a moment.

Absorbing the last drop through the tips of his fangs, he exhaled deeply and shrugged away a shred of tension. No amount of worrying could return his son, nor could it bring him closer to eviscerating his killer.

'He'll understand true pain once I've wrapped my claws around his windpipe,' he thought menacingly.

Geldam – noticing his goblet was empty – snatched a small server's bell and rang it vigorously, then returned his gaze to his cup. Golden gargoyles sat on three sides of it, intricately carved to match the ones placed on his castle's exterior. Everything within his home was chosen precisely to meet his lavish taste. The pale fern green walls of his study were wainscoted in gold, with thick molding surrounding the ceiling. He truly enjoyed the ornate.

He turned at the sound of the opening door.

"Bring me another bottle of wine, Xavier," Geldam commanded, holding his goblet aloft.

"I'm sorry, Geldam. I didn't bring any wine with me, although I can go tell Xavier you're thirsty," a feminine voice replied.

"Fiona?" Geldam said quizzically as she entered the doorway.

"I came here to offer my condolences, and also a favor," she answered.

Geldam eyed her impatiently as she strode across the room.

Fiona motioned to a tufted chair occupying another corner of the study. "May I?"

Geldam silently nodded in approval, and Fiona took her seat gracefully. She wore a tea-length dress patterned in a vibrant combination of gold and orchid blue. She always made a statement with her attire, the same way her host did with his decor. After she settled into her chair, Geldam's servant peeked into the room.

"I heard you ring, Sir," Xavier said.

Geldam raised his goblet. "I'd like another bottle of wine, and she'll have red tea with lemon and a snip of tarragon."

Xavier nodded politely and took his leave.

"Always the most gracious and knowledgeable host," Fiona noted with a smile.

"I try," Geldam answered in a melancholy tone, then turned his gaze away from her, staring moodily at the ornate stone fireplace.

"I heard from Adelina there's still no word from Davion," she said.

He eyed her with a single raised brow. "I thought I'd be receiving condolences, not an interrogation."

She lightly bowed her head. "I don't mean to be so forward, Geldam. Your son was taken too early, and it has left us all grieving. It's just that everyone in our House is frightened by that criminal lurking about the Midland."

Geldam's expression soured. He wanted to believe Fiona was being genuine, but he knew many in the Court were callous and opportunistic. Before he could reply, they were interrupted by Xavier.

"Here you are, Countess," he said while placing the saucer and teacup on a small end table next to her chair, "And yours, Sir," he continued, striding over and opening a new bottle of wine for Geldam.

Fiona stirred her tea with a small spoon a few times before taking a sip. She took an extra second to savor the contents before speaking. "Mmmm," she hummed soothingly, "I'm guessing the blood used for this tea was from Oxhathe humans?"

Xavier nodded. "Yes, Countess. The blood came from that region. Their diet of sweeter food is counterpointed by the citrus of the lemon and combines nicely with the licorice aromatics of the tarragon."

"Thank you for preparing such a wonderful beverage, Xavier," she complimented.

Xavier nodded appreciatively before striding out the large wooden door of the study. Geldam ignored their exchange, pouring himself another glass of wine after quickly downing his first.

Fiona watched the Count sigh after finishing a hefty sip.

"I believe you meant to say something," she said, noting his earlier expression after mentioning Davion.

Geldam shook his head. "It was nothing. You said your niece was curious about Davion's whereabouts. I know she fancies him."

Fiona barked a short laugh. "They entertain each other's company occasionally. I don't know if either fancy anything beyond the bedframe."

Geldam chuckled before taking another swig of wine. He set the weighty goblet down on his end table and straightened up. Spreading his hands, he asked, "Alright, Fiona, what's the favor you need from me?"

Fiona waved off his inquiry. "You misunderstand me, Geldam. I'm not looking for you to indulge a request of mine. I'm here to offer service to you."

Geldam bit his lip and eyed the countess. Fiona made him wait further as she took a lengthy sip of tea.

Finally, she set the cup down on its saucer. "If this criminal is as powerful as described, I'm worried Davion may not be enough. If he doesn't return, I'd be willing to lend you Tassia."

Geldam licked his lower lip nervously. Tassia was Fiona's lead Hunter and viewed as the most vicious Vampire in all of Vèspige.

He coughed away the anxious lump in his throat and spoke. "I doubt she'll be needed. Davion is more than capable. He's never failed a hunt before."

Fiona nodded slowly, acknowledging her colleague's point before replying. "I'm aware of Davion's reputation. However, it's been quite some time since he's hunted. Pardon me if you've shared this at a Court hearing, but did Davion ever explain why he stepped down from his post?"

Geldam turned his eyes to the fireplace, watching several flames lick the stack of wooden logs. "Belonging to the Court doesn't require divulging every private deliberation of my House."

She leaned back in her chair, giving him a warm smile. "I just want to ensure your House doesn't suffer more loss. Tassia would extinguish any further risk you carry…"

"Davion won't fail," Geldam interrupted gruffly.

A small pit of doubt festered in his belly, but he had to trust that Davion would return with his son's killer in tow. If he offered any others a Right of Hunt, the judgment would become a political game amongst the Royals that he didn't have the stomach for. He also wouldn't entrust the mission to such a bloodthirsty hunter as Tassia. Her methods often scorched the earth beneath her feet. She'd likely find a reason to rip the suspect's throat out rather than return him to Geldam in one piece.

Fiona finished her tea, then stood from her seat. "I know there's much on your mind, Geldam, so I won't trouble you further."

He stood and extended his hand to her, which she met with a gentle touch. He held her hand with both of his and nodded in gratitude. "I appreciate your offer, Fiona, but we at House Viruticus are resilient and cunning. That dastardly coward is no match for Davion," he stated optimistically, though his strained posture and puckered, grief-stricken eyes belied the words. Finished with his formal shake, he courteously opened the study door for her.

After passing through the frame, Fiona stopped and turned to face him. "Geldam..."

"Yes," he replied.

"I know you're eager to resolve this within your own House, but rumor says this man possesses magic the Court hasn't seen humans wield since the Waywards."

Geldam lifted his chin to respond, but Fiona cut him off.

"I know you're a proud man, Geldam. I just want you to know that out of respect for you, I'm leaving my offer open until Davion returns. For the first time in years, none of us know what we're dealing with here..."

CHAPTER TEN

"YOU'RE INSANE," he said, waving away what he'd just heard.

"If you untuck your tail for a bit, Davion, I think you'll find this is the only legitimate course of action," Carneth replied confidently.

Davion tugged on the reins to pull his horse to a trot. Carneth slowed Victor down to match his pace.

"Did you hear something?" Carneth asked.

Davion shook his head. "No, but we're reaching the next town in a few miles, so we need to finalize our plan."

Carneth held his tongue and waited for him to continue.

Davion eyed him. "Now you're silent? I assumed you'd snatch any opening to try and sell me on this preposterous idea of yours."

Carneth smiled at Davion, causing him to cough and look away. After discovering Carneth wanted to give his father – and former ally of Davion – a proper burial, Davion took the leap and revealed his secrets. The failed plan, the potion, and the fact that he was now trapped inside the very Court that stole his humanity. Carneth equally confided to Davion that his father, Regus, had told him how his Snare was removed. Davion thought Carneth would empathize with his plight and allow him to grab a sliver of redemption by inviting him to conduct a proper Wayward procession for Regus. Then they could leave Vèspige behind. However, he'd underestimated the arrogance of youth, especially one who strung together routine victories over Midland monsters.

'If you wish to honor my father – and your own order – let's find the bastard responsible for setting you up,' he'd eagerly proposed after hearing Davion's story.

Davion quickly countered him. *'I've been down that road for many years. The only one who knew anything was slain. Besides, the Royal Court is not an organization you can just waltz into, stab a few Vampires, and leave. Taking them on from the inside – just the two of us – would be impossible.'*

The two had continued back and forth, sparring over the decision to infiltrate the Court once more. Eventually, they both tired of the argument and rode silently through the night.

He didn't want to camp in the forest again, but he couldn't be seen with Carneth in any of the nearby towns until a solid plan was devised. Davion – his Vampiric vision not requiring daylight – noticed a side trail from the large dirt road and steered his horse onto it.

"Hey?!" Carneth called out as he yanked on his reins, trying to turn in time to follow him.

He held his lantern aloft while sending Victor in a gallop after Davion. Several yards down a tight dirt path lined with crimson spire oak trees, he found Davion tying his horse to a nearby tree branch. The area they occupied wasn't a nice clearing you'd typically camp in. This section was heavily wooded, cramped, and confining.

"You don't plan to camp here, do you?" Carneth asked, tying Victor to another tree nearby.

"We will if we can't come to a decision before daybreak," Davion explained, "I know you've had an impressive campaign while traveling through here, but what you suggested earlier is not some simple kill. If there even is anyone left to seek retribution from."

Carneth straightened up and crossed his arms. "You keep holding to the presumption that this Malnuvious was the only one involved. Don't you find it a bit peculiar that he was conveniently slain during that banquet along with your comrades?"

Davion frowned. "Of course I did. That's why I spent years searching for a hint of anyone living who was involved..."

Carneth held up his hands to carefully interrupt. "I know, Davion, you've told me everything you discovered during those years as a hunter. Is there any chance we could peel more information from Yaspen?"

"Don't confuse that merchant with an ally. I know you claimed he traded information for that mask, but he had other motives," Davion answered flatly.

"I understand he's not altruistic, no one would survive outside Qulàire's wall if they were, but he's clearly bent the ear of everyone with clout on this Intercontinent," Carneth argued.

Davion sighed and looked towards one of the cylindrical trees covered in red leaves. "Did you notice anything missing from Yaspen when you spoke?" Davion asked while casually plucking a leaf and rolling it between his fingers.

Carneth stared at Davion, confused at what he was supposed to have seen.

"If you look closely at his mouth, there's a couple of stumps where his fangs should be," Davion continued, "Do you think he lost them by whacking his mouth on a railing?"

Carneth raised an eyebrow.

Davion faced him. "The Court convicted him of a minor crime. They decided his punishment should be removing the only avenue to quench his incurable thirst, then banishing him to walk amongst the very humans he's incapable of feeding on. Let me consider how to describe it in terms you'd comprehend," Davion said, tapping his chin. After thinking for a beat, he stared at Carneth, raising a finger, "Drinking blood down your throat is like eating through your nose."

Carneth grimaced at the implicit visuals.

"That..." Davion continued, "was for a minor crime by one of their own. What treatment do you think they'd bestow upon us lowly humans?"

Carneth let out a heavy sigh. "Well then, there's only one way this can work..."

"Thank you for finally coming to your senses," Davion interjected.

Carneth wagged a finger at him. "Don't mistake those words for me giving in to your plan."

Davion buried his face in his palm. "Not this again. I can't tuck you away somewhere or sneak you into one of the Royal manors."

"Don't worry, Davion. I have no intention of hiding anymore or having you sneak me in," Carneth replied.

Davion's expression soured, fatigued with the carousel of failed ideas. "What is it then?"

Carneth stepped forward with his wrists pointed at Davion. "You'll bring me in as your prisoner."

"So, you can be eviscerated by Count Viruticus!?" Davion snapped.

Carneth returned a knowing smile. "He won't want to kill me when I explain that I was hired to assassinate his son by another member of the Court."

Davion's face twisted into an expression between confusion and epiphany.

Carneth continued. "Earlier, you said the Court was on the precipice of self-destruction before they united around the infiltration. Imagine how they'll react now. They're fat, happy, unobstructed, and content. Living an existence of ease and plenty. Their silky reality doesn't equip them to handle treachery of this magnitude. After the initial accusations finish flying, they'll begin sharpening knives for each other. Seeds of doubt blossoming into contempt. We won't have to look for answers, they'll fall into our lap. And if they don't, we'll just make our escape when the chaos truly begins."

Davion held his chin in contemplation as Carneth finished his argument, taking care to walk through a smattering of scenarios and consequences. Carneth's quick summation didn't give a complete picture. Sure, there was truth to it. If Carneth returned as a prisoner, jailed away from feasting fangs, they'd have a decent chance. However, it could just as easily backfire and send them both to an early grave. After minutes of deliberation, he finally made his decision.

Davion looked up from the ground at his new ally. "I know exactly which Royal member we should implicate…"

CHAPTER ELEVEN

TROTTING HORSEBACK along the weathered brick road, the messenger studied the night sky. He wished to rest but couldn't. Returning home to his wife before the upcoming holiday required him to maintain his blistering pace. Despite living on the road, Gremio made a point of being home with his love during a particular town festival. It commemorated their favored Spirit, Alrin, the god of enlightenment.

He had two letters, one from his boss, Yaspen, and another from a Witch out in the bogs. It wasn't peculiar that he delivered messages for Snared individuals, rather that two from such far reaches were sending word to the same person at the same time. He recalled his surprise at finding the same name scrawled across the Witch's letter as he turned it over in his hand. This wasn't someone powerful enough – at least in his opinion – to warrant this type of attention.

'Do you have any other runs before delivering that letter?' Yaspen had asked the week prior.

'I have one stop at the Witch Peregrine's home,' he'd replied.

Yaspen had raised a finger. *'Well, ensure that my letter is delivered before hers, regardless of the location. It's important this reaches him soon.'*

Remembering the interaction with Yaspen reminded him that his employer had no idea that this second letter was addressed to the same recipient.

Gremio reached over and unhooked the leather-bound canteen from his saddle. He sighed pleasantly after taking a hearty swig. The steel container held a mixture of juice, honey, and tea. His wife's recipe. Having brewed it at his previous campsite, it had finally cooled down enough to drink. Taking one more pull from the jug, he heard something large rustling in the woods to the east. Quickly shifting his reins, he took his horse off the trail and hid amongst a thick patch of white birch trees.

Gremio dismounted carefully onto the thick carpet of orange leaves, keeping their crunching down to a soft crumple. Reaching behind his back, he retrieved his broad axe. The tall single-bladed tool was a great weapon against any menacing creatures he encountered during his travels. Hiding behind an orange shrub, he snagged a vial from his belt and dropped a few bits of green solution into each eye, then blinked furiously against the stinging sensation prickling his irises. After enduring the brief pain, he peered around the bush with his temporary night vision.

"Peregrine never fails," he muttered aloud, squinting for a better view.

Aside from delivering her messages, stopping at the old Witch's home opened him to a shop of very useful survival potions. Gremio, still not seeing anything, decided to continue waiting anyway. Carefully untying the neck string for his cape, he gingerly tossed it over himself and part of the shrubbery. A wave of pale orange – like the shrub's leaves – washed over the cape like a gentle current, mimicking the plant life next to him. He left a small section uncovered so he could peek out into the darkness.

'It wasn't falling branches,' Gremio thought.

After several long minutes of waiting in dead silence, he finally noticed something matching his expectations. A pair of sunken yellow eyes hovered in the thick fog like two dissolving miniature pumpkins. With his enhanced eyesight, he noticed hanging brown skin covered in matted fur and four lanky appendages that stretched down to hooves tipped with short black claws.

'A ghoul,' Gremio said under his breath.

The monster was only slightly bigger than a mountain goat. It was something he could possibly fell, but he decided to remain hidden instead after realizing it didn't seem to be stalking anything in particular as it lurched into the clearing.

'I'll just wait it out,' he thought calmly.

"It's just a few yards further!" a burly voice shouted.

Several drops of lantern light bounced forward as the group of men loped towards the beast, surrounding it in a semi-circle. One of the men snatched something small and round from his waist and lobbed it into the air. The orb popped in a plume of orange sparks, casting light overhead equivalent to five lanterns.

'They clearly understand tactics,' Gremio noted.

Carefully positioning himself, one of the men swung a large sword at the ghoul's feet. With an awkward throaty howl, it lept back. The other three men made advances and took unsuccessful swipes of their own. As they fought, Gremio noticed their bulky leather clothing was lined with bits of lush fur. Perfectly designed for handling the cold temperature while also being sturdy enough to endure a battle with one of the smaller monsters lurking about the woods.

"Trappers," Gremio said quietly.

He watched as the group continued to attack the creature, but to no avail. It seemed this ghoul was quite agile. However, they would corner and slay such a small monster eventually. Gremio lowered himself onto one hip to survey the rest of the fight more comfortably. His assumptions were ill-timed.

The ghoul shrieked in anger, causing its dark fur to stand upright and shimmer like cast daylight. Then it grew. What was once the size of a farm animal swelled to the stature of a carriage. Gremio clenched his legs in fright as it morphed into a tall jackal with four finger-shaped claws.

The four men were unwavering – likely having fought many large creatures throughout their years – relentlessly swinging at their target. The monster hopped over one trapper, a heavy bald man with a long thin beard, and slashed a clawed paw through his back. The man wailed as he fell to his chest, blood rolling from his mouth. The creature snapped its head at the three remaining men and hissed, steam coiling from its flared nostrils.

"You'll pay for killing my brother!" a skinny trapper yelled as he charged forward, axe raised overhead.

His swing missed, clanging off a large rock and chipping his weapon. Gremio watched in horror as it snatched the man's arms and chomped into his throat. It seemed to savor the puncturing bite before ripping its jaw back, laying open its victim's neck. The last two trappers ran for the beast while it was still feasting on their fallen partner, hoping a team attack would give them a puncher's chance.

The monster accommodated them with two more grisly executions.

Gremio tried to stall his breathing, only letting oxygen escape his lungs in miniature puffs. Considering it had grown at will, he was fearful it might have keen enough senses to spot his visible breath in the cold winter night. He watched, wide-eyed, as the ghoul lapped blood from the fallen corpses.

After a few minutes, it seemed sufficiently satisfied and sat on its hind legs, waving a paw in front of its eyes. Gremio's face curled into an expression of sheer disbelief as the scruffy fur, claws, and jackal snout wafted away like scattered ashes.

A lone hooded figure silently occupied the clearing, now resembling a human form. Gremio held deathly still as it turned in his direction. It wore a mask emblazoned with slashes of crimson paint and thin slits for eye holes.

'*A hunting mask,*' Gremio thought.

Working with Yaspen let him peek behind the curtain where other humans remained blissfully naïve. Gremio remained in hiding but carefully retrieved a medal pinned to his chest that was shaped like the sun. It was given to him by Yaspen and represented his status as a messenger for the Snared, generally allowing him safe passage from hunts. Despite his clearance, he still gave the Vampire time to calm down from its bloodthirst.

'*Something about those markings seems familiar,*' he told himself.

He knew a few of the different Houses since Yaspen had scribbled some of the specific markings for him to study. It took a minute to place whose markings rested on the mask he currently witnessed. Then it hit him.

This was Tassia. The most feared hunter of all. More dangerous than any other employed by the Royals. She was also the most mysterious. No one knew her origins, and she never removed her mask, at least to his knowledge. If she wasn't employed by Countess Fiona, who held immense influence in the Court, it was unlikely they'd allow her antics. Tassia was known to be unforgivingly vicious and cared little for how much devastation she left behind. He'd heard from Yaspen that she'd slaughtered an entire town during a blood thirst. If it had been someone of lesser stature, they might have faced imprisonment for potentially revealing the Court's hunts.

Gremio watched her leap into the upper reaches of a tree and shriek a call to her fellow kind. When none responded, she gracefully hopped down and pulled off her mask.

"That's Tassia?" Gremio muttered in astonishment, "It makes sense considering who runs House Mayjere…"

Gremio waited as she licked the last droplets of blood from her gloved fingers. After adjusting a few straps of leather armor on her forearms, she placed the mask over her face and tossed her hood overhead. As she turned towards the road, a crackling branch caught her ear.

'Dammit!' Gremio gasped.

Despite his station as a courier for the Snared, he'd rather avoid interacting with someone as terrifying as Tassia, but there was no use hiding anymore. Still holding the sun emblem, he knew it would be safe to reveal himself now rather than cower suspiciously as she'd find him eventually.

"I'm Grem…"

Tassia darted in his direction.

Yellow sunlight blanketed Gremio as he pressed the medal between his fingers. Tassia leaped backward, throwing an arm over her eyes and hissing.

"I…I'm G…Gremio, a courier for Yaspen," he stammered.

Tassia took a few more steps away from the cylindrical curtain of light surrounding him.

"You've shown your allegiance… Now, please put out that damn light!" Tassia demanded.

Gremio lowered the medal, extinguishing the spell. However, for his own safety, he kept the magical object in his hand. Tassia climbed to her feet and rolled her neck, realigning herself after almost being struck by sunlight. Finally recovered, she continued her interrogation.

"What are you doing out here? Shouldn't you be traveling on the road?" she asked angrily.

Gremio crossed one arm and grabbed the other, hoping to stave off his nervous shaking. "At first I was, but then I heard fighting in the woods…"

"What did you see?!" she snapped before he could finish.

Gremio backpedaled, palms outfacing in surrender. "I only saw you walking amongst the dead," he belched in fright.

Tassia stood silently, observing the cowering messenger.

"Where is your next delivery?" she inquired.

Gremio swallowed the lump of terror in his throat before answering. "I...I'm heading to the Court. If you're done hunting, I'd welcome your company."

Tassia laughed. "No, no, no. I'd rather you retain your cover amongst the humans. A mere postman palling around with Court members might look suspicious, yes?"

Gremio noticed that even though her mask wasn't projecting anything, it seemed to alter her voice. Having delivered messages to the real person under it before, the voice he heard now was most decidedly different.

"Well, I'll be taking my leave then if I'm to return in time for the Ascension Day Festival," Gremio responded as he walked away, crunching across the forest floor.

"You celebrate Alrin?" Tassia asked.

Gremio looked over his shoulder at her. "Yes, my wife will be waiting for me."

"Ah. Well, offer her my condolences," she replied.

Gremio turned and observed her in confusion, eyebrow raised. "Condolences?" he replied quizzically, tightening his grip on the sun medal.

Tassia shrugged. "It's not easy traveling these roads for Yaspen. There are steep consequences for what you see out here, and I'm sure her heart weighs heavy every time you leave."

Gremio loosened his grip and nodded in agreement. "I'm sure she'll appreciate your empathy."

Gremio watched Tassia stride away gracefully, then turned on his heel and marched through the crackling branches and leaves. Only a few steps from his horse, he clipped the emblem back on his shirt.

Suddenly, a blunt force rammed through his midsection. He stiffened with shock, staring down at the clawed hand piercing his body. He was yanked backward and slammed into a tree, shattering what remained of his spine. Gremio slumped to the earth in a heap as the last sliver of life left his fearful eyes.

"Sorry, Gremio, I'm afraid you witnessed a bit too much on the road this evening," Tassia said while approaching his body.

She knelt beside him and diced a few more wounds into his body, leaving his corpse appearing as if it were mauled. She couldn't risk being revealed, but even more so, she couldn't raise suspicion if they knew she'd slain one of Yaspen's couriers. While he was banished from Vèspige and technically held no rights, Yaspen's merchant services had become so invaluable that attacking his men without reason wouldn't be accepted by the other Counts. And she didn't want to waste time crafting excuses before the Court.

Wind whirled through the trees, whipping Gremio's fur jacket open. Tassia noticed two beige envelopes peeking out from an inner pocket. She carefully plucked them from his clothing, turning them over in her hand to see who they were for.

"Davion?!" Tassia wondered aloud, "I'll save these for Fiona," she decided, sliding them into her hip pouch.

CHAPTER TWELVE

"ARE YOU SURE leaving me behind bars is necessary?" Carneth asked as the iron gates of his cell clanked shut.

"As I said earlier, this is the only way I can ensure you aren't devoured by Count Viruticus himself. Don't worry. I'll be free to return with food and water. There's no way the Court would let you die of starvation before having a chance at your throat," Davion explained calmly while locking the door.

"Duly noted. I guess the real question I should be asking is why you have your own personal jail out here," Carneth replied smugly.

Davion raised a finger. "If I'd found the one responsible for the death of my friends, I needed somewhere to store them that the Court couldn't trace. Additionally, when you become a Hunter, it's expected that you'll keep a few humans to yourself. Like an ice chest of sorts."

"Well, that should help me sleep at night," Carneth replied, crossing his arms.

Sliding the key into an overcoat pocket, Davion noticed Carneth raised an eyebrow in silent objection. His sardonic expression portrayed disagreement but also a complete lack of fear. Davion didn't understand how he maintained such confidence in his situation.

'Eventually, he'll face defeat like everyone else here, then he'll learn,' Davion mused, shooing away optimism.

"I thought you said no one knew about this location, and if someone finds me, I'd rather be free to defend myself," Carneth noted, interrupting Davion's thoughts.

Davion, who had walked towards the door, turned to face him. "Well, there is one Witch who's aware of this place, but she has no motivation to disclose its location nor any indication that you're staying here."

Carneth sat on a wood bench and leaned back against the stone wall. It was his only amenity aside from the small cot resting on the floor across from him. The cell was hidden beneath a cabin residing only a few miles from Peregrine's residence. It was a resting place for Davion when visiting the old Witch.

Davion continued. "Depending on how everything goes with the proceedings, I may actually leak your location and see what spills out."

Carneth leaned forward, placing his forearms on his knees. "So, if that decision is made, how do I avoid attack or capture?"

Davion pointed at Carneth's boot. "Use that vial of potion I gave you to become a Vampire. Considering your skill, I'd say that would offer you more than a fighting chance."

Carneth smirked. "Initially, I was excited at the prospect of using it. However, I recall you mentioning the potion only alters an existing Snare. I have not subscribed to that life yet."

Davion fingered his chin worriedly. How had he let that slip by him? He needed to offer Carneth some form of protection, but what?

"I'll leave your sword here," Davion answered, "I'll place it in my weapons cabinet near the stairs. If anyone attacks, you just need to reach it," he finished while pointing to a door at the end of the hallway.

Reaching through the bars, he handed Carneth a tan pouch made of thin fabric.

Carneth examined the pouch, turning it over. "And what's this for?"

"There's a few smoke and spark bombs in there. Enough to create the distraction you'll need to recover your sword," he answered while approaching the door.

Just before exiting up the stairs, he turned and looked at Carneth one last time. "Last chance, Carneth. If you'd like, we could gather what we need and flee to Qulàire or the Wolven Mountains…"

Carneth stood and wrapped his hands around the metal bars, ensuring he was as visible as possible to Davion.

"I won't run," he replied coldly.

Davion smiled. "Good, that's the spirit you'll need to survive what comes next."

"Davion has returned, Sir," Xavier said. Informing Count Geldam of the news he'd been anxiously anticipating.

The burly Vampire jolted from his opulent chair. "Bring him here immediately," Geldam blurted out, spittle flecking from his fangs.

Then, thinking better of it, he waved a pudgy hand at his butler before he could respond. "No, forget that order," he said, snatching a maroon pin-stripe blazer off its hook, "I haven't a moment left in me. I'll go directly to him. After what he's likely been through, I'm guessing he'll be resting in his quarters," he finished, hurriedly shoving his arms into his coat sleeves.

Xavier gave the conversation time to breathe before he handed the second bit of news to his employer. "If you wish to find him, you'll need to go to the assembly hall."

Geldam halted in confusion. "Why would he request to speak with me there?"

"He's not the only person awaiting your arrival," Xavier answered.

Count Geldam marched intently across the marble floor of the antechamber towards the main hall. As he approached the entrance, two servants spotted the arrival of their leader and quickly grabbed an ornate vertical handle on either side. The twelve-foot-tall doors were set on wheeled tracks and separated as the servants pulled them apart. Unlike his usual gravitas, Geldam didn't wait for the doors to finish rolling apart, instead sliding between them once enough room permitted. He observed everyone seated at the table, noticing it wasn't occupied by his men. Rather, it was the heads of other Houses.

'Mayjere, Gevistraut, Lonelle,' Geldam thought, noting each represented house while scanning the room.

At one of the head positions stood his own subordinate, Davion. Geldam slowly sunk into his seat at the opposite end from him, eyelids scrunched apprehensively while regarding his colleagues.

"Enough ogling, you lot. Davion, tell me where I can find my son's killer!" Geldam barked, crossing his arms impatiently.

Fiona watched the flustered Count with her ever-present half-smirk. Davion noted how amused she was at his superior's discomfort, then eyed the remaining guests. Most of them bore uncomfortable expressions of worry or discontent. Fiona seemed to be the only one unfazed by today's meeting. He'd broken the news to the attending Counts before Geldam's arrival. There was only one House yet to arrive, the most important one, House Elbourne.

Geldam looked at Davion for answers, and Davion shifted his eyes to the two empty seats. Geldam swallowed anxiously upon realizing they were waiting for Baron and Baroness Elbourne. Only one of the House's leaders was appointed to that rank, which was based on seniority. Baron and Baroness Elbourne had been Snared Vampires for longer than any of the Counts by several hundred years.

Everyone turned reflexively as the doors rolled open, then immediately showed respect by quickly standing to attention. The two highest Royals entered the room wearing long dark ankle-length robes. They were the only Vampires anyone knew with such control over their ability to glide that they could hover across the floor, only their toes touching the marble. Everyone else was relegated to fast dashes since they hadn't uncovered how to slow the ability down. The Elbournes also wouldn't teach them. The title of eldest Royal Vampire had to come with some advantages. Each of the House leaders made sure to ingratiate themselves with them in hopes of one day receiving their secrets. Supreme control of their gliding wasn't the only one they held.

Two servants hastily pulled Harker and Angel Elbourne's chairs out for them. Once seated, Harker instructed the servant to bring glasses of wine. The other remaining members took their seats and waited obediently for either of them to start the conversation. Davion studied Harker's inky black hair, gaunt features, and pale skin, which were blanketed by thick lavish robes. It was unnerving to see such a powerful entity bear the physicality of a starving vagabond.

Eventually, Harker lifted a slender finger, instructing Davion to continue. He steeled himself and addressed the crowd. Most of them already knew what he intended to disclose as he'd spoken with them before Geldam's arrival.

"I have captured Thadric's killer," Davion started, "However, I'm afraid after doing so, I could not bring him here."

Geldam's eyes widened, welling with rage.

Davion held up a hand showing scars on his forearm, hoping his explanation would stave off his leader's animosity. "I barely survived the fight, but after capturing him, he divulged a bit of disturbing information."

Geldam exhaled loudly and sank into his chair slightly, holding his tongue for the moment.

Davion bit his lip while observing him for a few seconds, then continued. "He claimed to be hired by one of our own..."

"WELL, WHO IS IT!?" Geldam shouted, slamming his fist on the table, unable to contain himself any longer.

Davion bowed his head, truly selling the moment before he revealed his hand. All the House heads glanced away, stared at their hands uncomfortably, or bit their lips nervously.

All except Fiona.

Davion scowled at her indifference, testing how she'd behave. She met his harsh gaze with a perturbed sneer, annoyed he was peddling his grief and Geldam's to her.

Davion sighed, looking at his superior directly. "The man claims you hired him, Sir."

Geldam's eyes lit with the same flame that once dwelled in his belly. "What preposterous nonsense is this?! Kill my own son? Now you're going to keep me from my rightful vengeance because that man accuses me of this utter absurdity. He's clearly forestalling his death sentence!" he yelled, rising from his chair.

Davion took a confident yet nonconfrontational posture.

"He states you planned to remove your successor and use this to instigate treachery amongst your enemies."

Geldam returned to his seat in a huff and slammed his fist against the table before burying his face into his palms. "I can't believe this is even being considered..."

Davion stood straight, holding his stance, wanting to seem as rational and impartial as possible to the other attendees, especially the Elbournes.

"I understand your anger, Sir. None in this room wants to withhold you from vengeance. However, the words of this man hold larger implications, even if they're simply a means of stalling," Davion explained.

The seated audience turned at once, unsure what Davion was implying. He'd only disclosed to them what Carneth had said beforehand. He hadn't divulged any of his own opinions or findings earlier.

"This man clearly knows names within the Court and the station of those he's killed," Davion continued, "If Geldam is not responsible – which I believe is true – then this killer is clearly working for someone else seated here," he placed his hands on the table, leaning forward, "and I intend to find out who."

CHAPTER THIRTEEN

"YOU CAUSED QUITE the stir among the Counts," Adelina slyly noted.

"It had to be said," Davion replied, picking bits of food for his plate from the buffet line, "The Counts have grown complacent with this easy life and want to ignore that one of their own is making a play for the throne."

Adelina laughed. "You're so dramatic, Davion. Really? A plot for the throne?"

She continued along the line as well, placing a few miniature fruit pies onto her silver-colored plate. Leaving room for him to refute her dismissal. Davion didn't answer. He finished selecting his food, then walked to the dining hall filled with circular tables covered in spotless white tablecloths. As was customary, each setting had a gold goblet and perfectly polished silverware. He found an unattended table and took a seat. Adelina followed and sat beside him.

"You don't need to sit alone, Davion," Adelina told him.

A servant arrived with a bottle. Davion observed the label presented to him and nodded approvingly. Once the server finished his duties of decanting the wine, they resumed their conversation.

"The Counts aren't happy with you, but you're not a pariah," Adelina continued.

He sipped port wine from his cup before taking a bite of sharp Toreseppé cheese – named after the town it was crafted in. Its pungency paired nicely with the full-bodied sweetness of his beverage.

"I'm guessing the blood for this wine came from Gilhem. It was Thadric's favorite place to hunt. He loved the sweet taste of its people. It's unfortunate he also met his end there," he critiqued quietly, ignoring Adelina's criticism.

She rolled her eyes. "Oh, come now. Don't feign affection for Thadric. He was an arrogant fool likely to meet an early end. He was incredibly careless with his hunting habits."

He looked up from his plate. "It's his wake, Adelina. Is there not one sympathetic bone in your body?"

She crossed her arms, observing another table. "I was hoping that joining you would spur a few others from our Houses to sit with us."

"Sorry to disappoint," he muttered.

Adelina's head snapped in his direction. "I don't understand your angle here. You call out the entire Court – in front of the Barons, might I add – only to sit here and sulk, despite not facing any repercussions for doing something so absolutely brazen."

He finished chewing another small cube of cured meat. "Maybe I don't have an angle, Adelina. Maybe I'm concerned one of our own is trying to remove opposition by creating violent conflict amongst certain Houses."

She sighed, picking a tiny pie from her plate and taking a nibble before speaking. "My sensibilities tell me I shouldn't be saying this, but I think there's something you should hear."

His eyebrows responsively raised at her vagueness.

She looked over both shoulders, then leaned close before continuing. "There is someone Countess Fiona and I have been quite suspicious of. We can speak further after the ceremony."

"Where should I join you?" he quickly replied.

Davion sat on a plush velvet chair in Fiona's study. The walls were lined with tall bookcases, some were open, and others had glass doors. He tried reading the spine of one of the many books filling the locked sections.

'House Recordings,' Davion noted, 'I'll have to find a way into that case sometime.'

His thoughts were interrupted as the study door slowly opened. Adelina entered first, wearing a black dress that fit her torso tightly but billowed out below the waist. She was followed by her aunt, Countess Fiona, who wore a slim, sophisticated beige dress that stopped at her ankles. She wore shiny black jewelry to accent the light color of her clothing, along with black boots.

Davion didn't customarily stand as she entered. Continuing to prod Fiona with little jabs, like ignoring her arrival, was an easy way to set her on her heels to start their conversation. Fiona noticed he was still seated, drinking his wine while distractedly observing the bookshelves. She didn't take kindly to being unnoticed. She turned towards Adelina with an incredulous frown. Her niece, just as perplexed by his lack of decorum, could only shrug and return a similarly confused expression.

Fiona took a seat opposite him.

"Something on those shelves interests you?" she interjected.

Davion hurriedly faced her, feigning being startled from a daydream. "No, Countess. Just lost in thought."

She returned a kind smile. "Yes, there must be so much on your mind after your tirade during that meeting. I'll have you know I spoke with Geldam and offered my full support. I even sent Tassia your way to help if things had gotten dicey there."

A reflexive lump of fear rose in his throat upon hearing that she'd unleashed her ruthless Hunter in his direction. Even if the gesture was well-intentioned, Tassia was a devious entity who took liberties whenever they came. Had he run into her during his travels, he and Carneth would likely be dead. Tassia had crafted excuses for her misgivings before but, due to Fiona's influence, hadn't faced any real consequences for them.

"I'm actually leaving to meet with her after our talk," she finished.

Davion set his wine glass down.

"I appreciate your help for our House, Countess," Davion cordially replied, "I hear you have some information you wish to share about suspicions within the Court."

Fiona leaned back in her seat and steepled her fingers confidently. "I'm suspicious of you, Davion…"

"Auntie, why are you accusing him?" Adelina interposed, "You told me House Lonelle concerned you?"

Fiona raised her hand, halting her relative's objection. "I only said that so you would convince him to join us here. Now, I need answers, Davion."

She rose from her seat, crossing her arms behind her back while approaching a glass case. "You took it upon yourself to find this... what was his name?"

"Carneth," he answered coldly.

"Ah, yes, Carneth. You captured him yourself, then decided to stow him away of your own accord and accuse everyone else of conspiracy. If you hadn't returned with that hunting mask he had, I doubt anyone would have believed you."

Davion glared at Fiona, but inside he was thrilled. The more she poked, the more leeway he had to directly accuse her later. He stood up defiantly and pointed towards the study window. "I barely survived out there trying to find that criminal. I won't tolerate such diminishment of my efforts!"

Adelina watched the two nervously. Davion noticed her concern and decided she really was put off by her aunt's accusations.

"Maybe Carneth isn't working for Geldam, but I wouldn't put it past him to work for you. It seems too convenient that you were able to hide him so easily," Fiona replied.

Davion tensely adjusted his coat. "I came out of retirement just so I could hunt that killer. I eventually brought him to his knees, and he confessed that last morsel of information to keep his hide attached. We both know if I brought him back here, he'd be slaughtered within one minute of reaching Count Viruticus, and none of us would know whether his words had merit."

Fiona tilted her head slightly and waved a finger. "Again, I find this all so peculiar. Last I heard from Adelina; you were a meager messenger whiling away your days in sullen solitude. Suddenly, you're bit with the nerve to hunt down the only human capable of killing our kind in nearly a decade…"

"Maybe I should ask why you're so quick to accuse me of malfeasance," Davion retorted, "I'm guessing it's easier to hide your own conspiring when you can distract any inquiries by publicly whipping me."

Fiona's face scrunched as she digested his retaliation. It seemed to have a bitter taste, but not strong enough to make her blurt out anything substantive. She took another quiet moment before replying. "I would suggest you remember who you're speaking with, messenger. Everyone humored your indictments out of respect for the circumstances that led us here, but if you continue to disrespect me, your little game ends right here in this room."

Davion shivered and took his seat once more, knowing that showing signs of heeding her intimidation opened her up to his next jab. Fiona smiled thankfully and took her seat as well.

"So," she continued, "without leaping to anger, convince me why I shouldn't suspect you're angling to benefit from this Carneth situation."

His posture stiffened. "I was nothing before Count Viruticus gave me an opportunity. I went from scrounging the alleys of the Midland to leading his Hunts. This mission meant more to me than vengeance. It was repayment for everything he's offered me. Which is why I was extremely troubled by that man's words," Davion leaned forward in his chair and clasped his hands, "I know Count Viruticus is not responsible, and I would be foolish to simply ignore how informed and coordinated all of Carneth's movements have been. I believe there's something more going on here."

Fiona held a finger to her chin, noting his response. "I can understand why you'd believe that. However, most of my colleagues are in alignment that he's toying with you to keep himself alive."

He took a hearty swig from his glass and sighed. Holding his tongue to let the conversation breathe. Fiona's presence was incredibly unnerving, which made it easy to play at being fearful of her.

She sat confidently, ankles crossed, observing him. "I believe you're sincere here, but I'm worried you're well above your station. Carneth's words have caused enough havoc within the Court because you refused to maintain your composure. Lambasting all of us in front of the Baron and Baroness created unneeded tension amongst the Counts and Countesses," she stated.

Reaching to her side, she pulled open a drawer from her end table, then retrieved a pen and paper. He watched intently as she scribbled a quick note.

"This is a direct message from me," she said, handing him the slip of paper, "If you need counsel with me during your investigation, please show this to my servants, and you'll be seen immediately. I've always been an ally of House Viruticus, and I'll do everything I can to assist you."

Davion took the note and held it in both hands. "Thank you, Countess. I know you've aligned well with our House, and I apologize if my temper offended you. Maybe being appointed as a special inquirer for this investigation by Baron Elbourne has me on edge. We both know he won't accept failure after assigning me to such an important role."

Davion watched Fiona's cloying smile slide off her face. He knew she wouldn't like being reminded how that meeting was adjourned, with the Baron himself granting Davion a temporary title that gave him complete oversight of the investigation.

She returned his comments with a begrudging smile. "I think you'll do just fine on your own... for the moment. Eventually, when you need guidance from someone experienced at bending the ears of high-ranking Royals, I'll be happy to assist."

Davion stood and bowed slightly at her supposed gesture, which he knew in actuality was a charge against his competency. However, he refrained from engaging in another argument, wanting to save his next question until the last possible moment.

Fiona looked at Adelina, who opened the door for them.

"Would you mind if I personally escorted you to your carriage, Davion?" Fiona asked.

He smiled and extended a bent arm to her cordially. "Of course, Countess."

As they strode through her manor, arm in arm, Davion noticed she was taking a longer route to reach the front entrance.

'Clearly, she wants all her subordinates to see us appearing as a united front,' he noted.

Finally reaching the immense arched doorway of Mayjere Manor, Fiona placed a hand on Davion's back.

"I know you were trying your best, Davion, but after all the time you've spent with Adelina, I would've hoped you could have confided in her and used my influence to deal with this in secret. If there really is a culprit, it's going to make it nearly impossible to find answers now."

"Well, there's no reversing course," he said solemnly as her servants opened the doors for them.

He took a step to leave, then stopped himself. He'd saved his best test for last.

"There is something I'll need your help uncovering," he said.

Fiona interlaced her fingers gently, taking on a curious expression.

He continued, "Carneth mentioned something very troubling during my interrogation. He claimed to be searching for one of the Waywards. Stating there was one more culprit who helped organize that plot who's still hiding within Vèspige."

"Do you believe him?" she replied, quickly deflecting the question back onto him.

He scratched his chin. "After they infiltrated our ranks with Malnuvious during his attempt to take the throne, I'm worried it's entirely possible."

Her face grew cold and expressionless before she waved off the notion. "That's impossible. Those potions only granted them a temporary veil to disguise themselves. And the House linked with leading that treachery was wiped from this Intercontinent."

"I thought the same. However, maybe there was more than one House involved in concocting that potion?" he asked aloud.

She held her firm posture but was clearly distressed by his remarks. "I'm not sure what I should do with such a preposterous statement, but I'll see what I can uncover."

He bowed before making his way down the grey stone steps towards the carriage she'd arranged for him. Upon reaching the door, he turned and waved to her one final time.

"Countess," he called out.

She stepped through the threshold onto the landing to better hear him.

"I heard he communicated with Yaspen. Maybe there's something you can find out by speaking with him," he said before stepping inside the carriage.

Looking through the small window, he watched Fiona turn on her heel and march back into her castle. As his carriage rolled back to castle Viruticus, he reviewed their conversation internally.

Suddenly, a fact spilled to the front of his consciousness.

'How did she know with such certainty that the potion was only temporary with humans?'

He smiled to himself, knowing he finally had the first credible lead in several years.

'Now, I wonder what she'll inevitably confide to Yaspen. That merchant is impeccable at prying at least a few secrets from everyone he meets.'

CHAPTER FOURTEEN

YASPEN SET HIS glass of rum down on a nearby barrel. He leaned against the front desk of his lobby, staring out the square front windows. He'd received word from one of his messengers that a visitor requested a personal meeting at his outpost in Elmweir. It was a prosperous trading town just outside the western swamps. Witches and Warlocks looking for ingredients helped the economy thrive, while their power made the city safe from Vampire hunts.

'The magic of this town is truly splendid,' Yaspen thought, staring at the lanterns hovering over the doors of every business   outside.

It was finally nightfall, which was why he was downstairs in the front lobby rather than withdrawn into his upstairs office. Despite his fangs being ripped from his jaw, he still had the same weaknesses as his kind. He also couldn't untether his Snare, as only humans – when they wielded that power – had gained the ability to remove it. Vampires, Werewolves, Witches, and Warlocks, were given the best gifts the Spirits could offer but were eternally imprisoned in Moncroix for it.

"If I'd returned as a Warlock, I wouldn't feel like I'm starving every waking moment," Yaspen grumbled, recounting the cave where he'd accidentally uncovered traces of the Spirit that Snared him.

He downed the last gulp of his dark syrupy coffee. It quelled – for now – his insatiable thirst for blood, taking the edge off for at least a few hours. The rum he distilled worked even better, but he was saving that for his next craving. He was unable to suck enough spilled blood through the stumps in his mouth to offset the inevitable intoxication. Maybe if he'd had more food in his belly, that would help, but Yaspen didn't enjoy eating immediately upon waking. No, with this visitor, he needed all his physical and mental faculties at their pinnacle. Of all the Royals, he hated – and feared – this visiting one the most.

"Fiona, dear," Yaspen said cordially, stepping around his desk.

He met her in the foyer, reaching both hands to hold one of hers. She smiled at his courteous gesture. Even if it was a customary façade, she relished the idea of Yaspen being forced to show her such affection.

"Please, join me in my quarters," he said, motioning her to follow.

The two strode around his desk, taking the stairs to his private office.

"I see your business is doing well these days, Yaspen," Fiona acknowledged upon seeing the elaborate décor.

Two of the chairs were made from Rhinox leather, a beast hailing from the Intercontinent of Malcozé. The other seating was comprised of benches covered in shiny maroon fabric. Thick trim etched with wavy patterns vertically adorned the wall every two feet. The last quarter section of each wall before reaching the ceiling was painted with scenes of various historical figures reenacting a pivotal moment from their past.

Across from the entry were two sets of open shelving from floor to ceiling covered in various trinkets. Fiona elegantly strode towards them across the wood floor, partially covered in a beautifully patterned rug. She leaned close to one shelf, observing one item in particular.

"Is that a conjuring staff?" she asked, pointing to it.

"Yes, that was given to me by a Witch I often trade with," he replied, stepping beside her and lifting it, "They're like snakeskin, actually. The magical properties eventually leave, and the user sheds them for a new one," he said, holding it flat in both hands.

The slim gnarled stick curled into a snail shell circle at its top and was pointed at the bottom. He raised it vertically so the pointed side was down, then jabbed it against the floor. A gem at the center of its circular top glowed mucus green for a fleeting moment, then dimly extinguished.

Yaspen handed Fiona the staff. "You see, its inherent magic has departed."

The Vampire Countess took it, then proceeded to turn it over in her palms. "Did this come from Peregrine?" she asked.

Yaspen raised an eyebrow but held his response. Fiona looked at him knowingly, then handed it back. She didn't need to press further about its previous wielder; his silence spoke for him.

"Would you like some coffee?" Yaspen asked, breaking the silence, "I have a fresh batch simmering."

Fiona observed him, thankfully. "Yes, that would really help stave my thirst. I've been deprived since last night."

Yaspen's lips pursed as she eyed him cheerily, dragging her tongue along one fang. He didn't enjoy her chiding reminder that she could quench her bloodthirst willingly. He choked down his animosity and leaned his head out his office door, calling for a servant downstairs. After a few minutes, a short, stocky fellow in a buttonfront shirt delivered two freshly poured mugs resting on saucers.

"You know, Yaspen, sitting here, I actually find myself envious of you," she said after finishing a slow sip.

"How so?" he asked, his mug clinking lightly as he returned it atop its saucer.

"You can mingle amongst them, employ them, travel anywhere you want across the Midland, carefree in the knowledge you won't be driven to the indulgence of puncturing their neck," she scoffed, casually observing his servant who still stood by the door obediently.

Yaspen turned and noticed he was fearfully gawking at Fiona. He snapped his fingers to gain the servant's attention, then waved him away. The servant nodded in acknowledgment, then hastily retreated downstairs.

Yaspen sighed, slumping his chin into his open hand. "Is it necessary to intimidate everyone the first time you meet them?"

"Why shouldn't I?" she inquired, "We should relish these gifts from the Spirits. A sprinkle of healthy fear won't harm him. It should make his loyalty to you that much stronger, knowing what awaits him without your protection."

Yaspen silently regarded her while taking another drink. Rising from his chair, he walked over to the rectangular window behind his desk and drew apart the curtains, surveying the street below.

"What would you like to know about Carneth?" he asked calmly.

"Right out with it then," she chortled, setting her drink down, "Actually, I wanted to ask you about Davion."

Yaspen bit his lip, continuing to face away from her, merely turning his head. "Yes?"

Fiona smiled and drew a finger to her chin. "It seems the two of you correspond regularly. I'm surprised he'd have the funds to purchase from you so often?"

"He doesn't," Yaspen countered indignantly, "Davion is a lonely man, Fiona. Why do you think he took the messenger position for Geldam? I don't know what tortures his soul, but I'm sure you've seen him brooding about, considering your niece is another form of relief for his lack of meaningful companionship."

Fiona raised an unimpressed eyebrow, her lips twisting into a frown of their own. "Even if that's so, why would he bother you? His weapon is likely better than anything you peddle."

Yaspen stepped away from the window and took a seat in his chair, positioned behind the rectangular wood table he used as a writing desk.

"He came to me for information, just like all you Royals do. Despite casting me amongst the humans, I've accomplished more than anyone in your aristocratic ranks," he stated flatly.

She laughed. "You... more accomplished? If you knew what it took to get the Hunting grounds established, I believe

131

you'd bow and thank me," she finished by pointing a slender finger at him, her sharp nail covered in black paint.

"I..."

She pulled her hand upright and wagged the same finger to interrupt him. "Before you whine about those missing teeth, remember that these grounds built the foundation for you to prop up your little establishment. The need for which would be extinguished if the humans went back to viewing us as enemies again."

He crossed his arms. "Merchants are always necessary. No matter which political structure is erected. Ultimately, the market dictates everything."

She leaned forward to argue further, then thought better of it, relaxing her posture and settling back into her seat. "So, Davion came to see you about Carneth..."

He nodded. "Yes, he wanted to know if I'd come across the boy, which I had."

Her eyes grew wide, but she didn't interject, hoping he would elaborate further if she yielded him the floor.

He smiled at seeing her unspoken gesture and continued. "Davion demanded I disclose our conversation, which I did out of respect for the Court. I informed him Carneth is a young man who came here on a fruitless search, which led him to work with your kind."

"Who exactly is he working with?" she asked.

He shook his head. "He wouldn't tell me exactly who, just that it was someone in connection with removing the Waywards..."

She pressed a tongue to one fang, digesting his words before pressing further. *'Only Malnuvious and I built that trap.*

After he took the fall, there's no one left of his House to seek vengeance on me, is there?'

She ran every related noble through her mind and couldn't recall anyone alive that was aware of their secret.

"Did I offend you, Fiona?" Yaspen interrupted.

She blinked away her thoughts and folded her hands together. "Just recalling the fear of fighting them that awful night. Tell me, did Davion inform you that Carneth supposedly claimed to have been hired by Geldam."

"Why would Geldam slaughter his own son?" he asked.

She sighed. "It seems like a ploy to create tension that distracts us from executing him. At least, that's what most of us believe. Davion seems convinced that Carneth is working with another Count."

He licked his lower lip in contemplation. "It's possible. When I spoke with him, he had a Hunting Mask in his possession."

"Where is it?" she snapped.

He cocked an eyebrow. "It's secured safely in my possession.

She uncrossed her ankles and leaned forward, pointing an accusatory finger at the merchant. "That's Court property; you're required to hand it over immediately."

"Don't worry, Fiona, I planned to hand it over," he answered.

The edge of her thin lips curled in annoyance. "I'm appointed as the steward of that equipment since I'm the only one capable of crafting them."

"Well, I'm sure once I've delivered them to the Baron, they'll be disseminated accordingly," he replied smugly.

133

"You're barred from his presence. Anything you send to him can only come through one of us. If the law didn't allow the Counts to trade with you, your business would be bankrupt," she snapped.

"I'd argue that your lot trades with me out of necessity, although you mostly shop for answers and rarely purchase anything..." pausing, he regarded her contemptuous stare and decided to move forward with his reasoning rather than belabor this specific point any further. "Considering the severity of the situation, I felt it best any evidence be submitted to the highest authority."

Frustrated, she turned her head away. "I'm surprised you didn't give it to Davion, considering the Baron gave him authority over this investigation."

"He doesn't know I have it. Only you're aware at this moment," he answered.

Her dour sneer rose into a smile. "I appreciate your willingness to save such vital knowledge for me."

"Since your House crafts them, I actually hoped we could deliver it together," he said.

She lifted her chin curiously. "Why involve me now?"

He raised his hand, palm facing her. "As you said, it's illegal for me to approach Baron Elbourne. You can deliver it in my stead."

She shrugged expectantly. "I can take it off your hands now if you'd like?"

He rubbed his chin. "Unfortunately, I don't have it stowed here. I left it at the outpost where I met Carneth. It's being watched to ensure a proper chain of custody."

She bristled. "You're taking every formal step; I'm actually impressed."

He shrugged and tilted his head. "I think you'll understand why it's necessary to do so once you've seen it. I won't open myself to the slightest possibility of incrimination," upon finishing his thought, he stood from his chair. "Is there anything else I can offer?"

"I think you've given me enough," she silkily replied, rising from her seat.

Touching a finger to his temple, he lightly saluted her, then extended a palm towards a dresser with a few small boxes stacked on top. "May I offer you any treats to take home? I've received a new batch of tarts from a distinguished Qulàire bakery that hasn't reached my shelves yet. They're in the boxes on top."

She grinned. "If you could spare a box, that would be lovely."

Yaspen selected one at the top of the stack before opening the door for her. He handed it over as she made her exit. Watching her descend the stairs, he waited for the bronze bell at the front entrance to chime before shutting his office door.

"You're safe now," he said coolly.

A solitary bookcase slid from its position, and a lone man stepped forward. "I appreciate your cooperation, Yaspen."

Yaspen waved him off. "If you hadn't shown me that badge Baron Elbourne gave you, along with a letter from Fiona herself, I'd have sent you away before you could blink."

Davion laughed while straightening his hip-length coat.

"As you saw yourself, she's the one who insisted I take that letter allowing me direct counsel anytime I desired."

Yaspen cocked an eyebrow. "Will she believe that this meeting falls under those terms?"

Davion adjusted his shoulders, stretching them after being cramped in his host's hidden closet. "I'm sure we'll never reach that point, Yaspen. Now, tell me about this Hunting Mask you've acquired."

Yaspen strolled back to the leather chair he had occupied earlier, took a seat, and drank another sip of coffee. Davion eyed him impatiently.

Yaspen looked up from his cup, confused. "Didn't you receive my letter?"

"I must have left before it arrived," Davion replied.

Yaspen shrugged. "Like I told her, you'll see that Mask as soon as the Baron does."

Davion crossed his arms. "You're really taking this seriously."

Yaspen leaned back after finishing another drink. "Of course I am. Now, I'd like to know why Carneth is suddenly spouting off stories about working with the Court. After meeting that boy, I was under the impression those killings were of his own accord."

Davion didn't answer, biting his inner cheek to hold back a telling grin.

Yaspen squinted harshly. "Toying with Counts is foolish enough, but adding Fiona to this mixture – it's beyond dangerous. You're dangling a torch over dry wood, my friend."

Davion smiled. "It's good to know my status has risen above customer."

Yaspen threw his arms up, rising from his seat. "Now you drop the sullen routine and start cracking jokes?"

136

Frustrated, Yaspen approached his window again. Despite it being nightfall, carriages and townsfolk traveled along the well-lit cobblestone streets. This town was one of the few places rid of monsters, forbidden from hunts, and void of any influence from the venomous Vampires who secretly ruled over many nearby villages. Aside from the economic benefits of this location, placing his base of operations here provided a safe haven. Staring at the town below eased his nerves.

"What have I walked into here, Davion? What are you really after?" Yaspen asked, hands clasped behind his back.

Davion didn't answer. Instead, approaching the boxes of treats Yaspen mentioned earlier, he shuffled through them until he reached one at the bottom. Opening it, he selected a chocolate truffle with fudge and ground coffee filling. Yaspen looked over his shoulder grudgingly, impressed despite himself at his guest's cavalier attitude. Davion hummed happily as the grounds in the confection's center eased his bloodthirst.

"Don't fret, Yaspen. I only wish to prune a few rotten limbs from our Royal tree," he replied before licking up the last morsel.

CHAPTER FIFTEEN

"THIS STAFF IS ONLY a year old, Davion," Peregrine explained, stirring one of her cast iron cauldrons.

Her conjuring staff had a similar makeup to the expired one she'd let Yaspen keep. Of course, a Witch would tell you that no two staffs are the same, that each possesses unique characteristics, and that any wielder worth her salt could easily tell them apart.

"I don't buy it. It even has the same curling knot at the top with the green gem," Davion replied casually, leaning back and resting an arm over the top of his chair, "I think you handed Yaspen a fake so he'd believe your story. Witches love hoarding secrets from the rest of us. Then once we're close to discovering one, you spread misleading lore."

"Hmph," Peregrine sniffed, obviously displeased.

She lifted the staff from the mixture and gave it a solitary shake, sending light-blue goop back into the bulky pot.

"Aren't you here a bit early?" she asked.

Davion smiled. "You know I always stock up early. Soon though…"

"You'll be able to buy the recipe from me," she interrupted, finishing his thought.

"I actually meant to say I won't need it," he said confidently.

Peregrine stopped her stirring, glancing at him. "You found someone who can break your Snare?"

"He claims to be able to. I won't know for sure until I uncover who else in the Court crafted the plot to kill my brothers," Davion answered, sighing.

"That's his price, eh?" Peregrine smugly said. "I hope he's being honest with you. Whether this fails or succeeds, one thing is certain; you'll never be able to return to Vèspige again."

She scooped a hunk of the mixture out of the cookpot with a smaller steel pot and set it on top of her oven. Grabbing a handful of powder that looked like grey and gold salt, she threw it inside the oven and shut the door. A three-inch flame erupted from a hole atop it, which Peregrine placed her pot over. Eventually, the goop boiled down to a drinkable liquid, which she poured into several vials set in a wooden holder.

"That doesn't look like the usual batch?" Davion asked, standing from his seat to get a better look.

"I told you each staff is unique. I have to adjust my methods a bit since it's his first time," she grumpily answered.

"His?" Davion asked.

"Each one lives and breathes Moncroix air after it's passed our rigorous testing. Earning themselves a name," she answered while drizzling a red, sappy substance into each vial.

"What's his name then?" he asked.

139

Peregrine shook her head. "Afraid if I told you, then you could command him. He's so young that I need him to know only one master."

Davion poured himself a cup of tea before taking his seat.

"The Warlocks don't seem to get so worked up about their staff," he said, smirking.

He lept back as flame plumed in his direction. He saw Peregrine, fists on her wide hips, glowering at him.

"The stuffy Warlocks would wield better magic if they took time to understand their vessels better," she scoffed indignantly before turning back to her row of vials, "bunch of snobs, that lot."

Davion climbed to his feet, laughing. "So sensitive."

His host grumbled under her breath while applying the finishing touches to her recipe, then pushed a cork into the top of each vial.

"I'm not sure how I feel about this plot, Davion," she said, walking away to grab herself a cup of tea as well.

He took the vials and placed them into a satchel. "I think you're just sad I'll be gone."

"You've got miles ahead before you're through with the Court," she answered solemnly.

Davion smiled. "After the many years I've spent trapped within their ranks, this won't feel long at all."

Tassia watched from above as Davion left Peregrine's home. Preparing herself, she snatched a thin vial of blood from a belt that crossed her chest. She waited for him to emit a Vampiric call. Unlike most animal calls, it wasn't for help but rather to alert others of their kind to feast. The call sent an impulsive urge through any Snared Vampire to race towards it. Hearing his cry, she swept one hand over her mask. The action cast a translucent spell around her that dampened noise.

Tassia was fortunate that her mask was created by Fiona, who ensured it was enhanced with magic the other Royals lacked. Jabbing a fang through the vial's wax seal, she slurped the blood next. Even after her most protective precautions, the call still sent a thumping sensation through her core, begging her to come. The call was an instinctual necessity in the days when Vampires were alleyway parasites, crawling through life salivating for their next meal. In their current standing of pack hunting and secret rule, the call was only used for detection or cries for help.

Steadying herself against the solid tree limb, Tassia took a moment to collect herself. After meeting Yaspen in Elmweir, Fiona believed Tassia should visit Peregrine. Luckily for her, she spotted Davion leaving the city and trailed him to a hideout not far from the Witch's home.

'I'm sure that's where he's hiding Carneth,' she thought, *'Once this Witch tells me why she's conspiring with Davion, I'll collect him next.'*

"It's nice to get two visits in a row," Carneth said, smirking.

Davion rolled his eyes and grabbed the bowl of minced potatoes, scooping a helping onto his plate.

"For a creature that should only desire bloodsucking, you certainly know how to make a good meal," Carneth continued before taking a bite of roasted carrot.

"Blood is only what we… what Vampires crave. It's like water to them. But unlike water, it's an intoxicant as well," Davion replied before stabbing a fang into a raw piece of steak.

Carneth watched him suck every last drop from the slab of meat until it turned grey. "Does animal blood do the trick? Is that how you avoid leaping for my throat?"

Davion plopped the steak onto an empty plate. "Imagine you're walking through the desert, stranded in the heat. You come upon a beautiful woman who presents you with a stone-cold glass of water. It not only slakes your thirst but rejuvenates you. Gives you a renewed sense of vigor to charge through that desert until you escape. That…" Davion said while snapping a bite of carrot in his mouth, "is live human blood. This…" he grabbed another wet slab of raw steak and guzzled its crimson juice with two fangs, then tossed it aside, "is that same glass of water. But instead of fresh and cold, it's covered in dust and tepid because someone drank half then left it in their musty house for days."

"Point taken," Carneth said under his breath before returning to his food. He paused after a few bites, then glanced up at Davion again.

"What now?" Davion asked incredulously.

"After hearing your lovely analogy there – I'm curious – if human blood is like an intoxicant, do you ever reach the peak you started with? Or are you constantly chasing after it?"

Davion took his time chewing his food. Not for the need to deliberate on Carneth's words but because he felt like making him wait.

"It's just as good every time, if not better," he finally answered.

Carneth took a sip from his stemmed wine glass, then spoke. "Well, on that note, maybe I should return to my cage."

Davion rolled his eyes at Carneth's hackneyed attempt at levity, then rose from his chair and walked towards the small kitchen.

"Would you mind grabbing another bottle? I really want to indulge myself before you lock me up again," Carneth called, shaking an empty wine bottle.

Tassia sauntered across the large slabs of white limestone that led to Peregrine's home. She halted after reaching the final step before the front porch, noticing warm light glowing through the windows. The house came to life, the window frames blinking as its siding below opened like a mouth. Sounds of roots snapping and digging dirt emitted as it lifted itself onto two stumpy peg legs.

"Why have you come here?" the building boomed.

Tassia carefully stepped backward, avoiding furtive movements. "I come here to purchase from Peregrine," she replied calmly.

The window eyes frowned. "Do not lie to me, Vampire. I do not recognize you."

"That's because we haven't had the pleasure of meeting yet," she answered, opening her arms politely.

The living cottage hummed uncomfortably.

"I am given the faces of those she trusts. You are not one of them," it answered through gritted teeth made of wood planks.

Tassia looked down, adjusting her elbow-length gloves. "I guess I'll have to find her myself then."

The living home growled at her threat, tree trunk arms emerging from its sides. It swiped for her with a branched paw. Expecting the attack, she rolled away gracefully. More grabs for the nimble Vampire followed, but she easily avoided them as well.

"Tell Peregrine to come out, or I'll have to take the offensive," she quipped, skidding to a stop after evading another swing of tree limbs.

"You underestimate me, little Vampire," it said in a baritone voice, its peg legs growing another story in height.

Tassia hunched, readying herself.

"Let's see how fast you can run," it said, smiling a wooden-tooth grin.

Eyes growing wide behind her hunting mask, she turned and fled. Hunks of dirt, roots, and swamp grass spurted up and were flung behind the monstrous structure as it chased her. Murky swamp water splashed at Tassia's feet as she rounded a corner behind an immense tree. Its circumference at least fifteen times her own. A thunderous crack rang out as the tree split some twenty feet above her.

"Dammit!" she yelled, rushing for cover behind the next tree.

Somehow it hadn't seen her hide through the explosion of rotting wood from the last one it attacked. Back pressed to the trunk, she caught her breath as it lumbered about in search of her.

'I have to get inside,' she told herself.

Looking up, she saw the hefty branches of the tree she stood against were well above her leaping ability.

"I warned you, Vampire," it called out, "Come out and face your penance for trespassing on my master's grounds."

'I don't have much time. I need to reach those upper branches,' she thought, glancing around.

'There,' she said, finally spotting the way.

She retrieved a vial from her hip pouch containing a magma-like substance and poured it onto a dagger. Running across the ankle-deep water, she headed for a ten-foot tree tipped over and resting against a large boulder. It was the closest thing to a catapult she could find.

She threw the blade – now covered in bright-orange heat – at a similar-sized tree ahead. It melted the trunk, sending it crashing down onto the opposite end of the one she stood on, smashing it like a fist pounding a table. Now shot across the murky grey sky, she elegantly back-flipped onto a higher limb in one of the massive trees she'd hidden behind earlier.

Staring from her new vantage point, she saw the cottage glaring up at her with luminous pollen-yellow windowpane eyes.

"Rraaahhh!" it thundered, growing its legs again.

A large hand of bark-covered fingers clawed for her. Rather than flee, she dove forward into the behemoth's attack. Slicing ahead like an arrow, she crashed through one of its windows. Tucking at the last minute, she rolled safely to a kneeling position on the wood floor. Quickly turning to face the interior of the room, she readied herself for combat, guard up and claws extended.

"I thought you just came here to buy something?" Peregrine chortled, sipping a cup of tea at her kitchen counter.

Tassia stood slowly, adjusting the leather armor covering her torso. "You'd have my money by now if I wasn't distracted."

Peregrine cackled. "Don't take it to heart, dear. My pup barks at everyone on their first visit."

"I'd say he does a fair bit more than bark," Tassia retorted.

Peregrine shrugged and poured herself another cup.

"What do you seek? I have a few powders in stock you'd probably..."

"I come here for answers," Tassia interjected, "and I'm happy to exchange coin for them."

Peregrine chuckled as she took a seat behind a small round table covered in knick-knacks. "Oh... well, I'm not much for gossip these days, dear, so I doubt I'll have much worth sharing. Go on and ask, though."

Tassia lowered her hood but left her hunting mask on. Her hair was tied back in a bun, and waves of clear teal smoke billowed from her mask. As their conversation continued, the house wobbled back and forth, its legs carrying them back to their original resting place.

"What potions is Davion buying from you?" she asked, tossing a coin purse on the Witch's table.

Peregrine eyed the bag, then took another sip of tea.

"Take that mask off, and maybe you'll gain my trust."

Tassia laughed, placing a thumb on her chin. "I think you misread the room, Witch. You will take the bargain, or you won't make any more."

Peregrine snorted. "Child, many people – much more powerful than you, I might add – have come here making demands," she stood from her chair and grabbed a small wand off the wall, "Not one has succeeded."

Tassia smirked, hands on her hips. "I'm surprised you didn't grab the bigger one by the cauldron."

"We both know magic comes in many forms, and the most powerful forms are always the most concentrated." Lifting the wand as she finished, it snaked itself around her hand and wrist like a dark vine.

Tassia reached behind her back with both hands, stuffing her fingers through a set of pearlescent knuckles. "You're right about that... dear."

Peregrine shot a cluster of vines at Tassia, who sidestepped them. Tassia dove forward, slamming into the Witch's chest forearm first. Her momentum sent them crashing through the wall, and wood splintered around them. Spiraling mid-air, hands around each other's throats, they fought viscously. Peregrine coiled ivy around Tassia's neck and arm – and Tassia, in turn, slashed Peregrine's face. Broken earth exploded around them as they struck the ground like a tangled missile.

Tassia tumbled for several feet, eventually coming to a stop on her side. Pulling herself to rest on one arm, she looked over at Peregrine, lying on her back like a plump starfish. Tassia staggered a bit from the impact as she reached her feet. The Witch sat up and howled with laughter. Tassia watched as the slashes on Peregrine's pitted cheeks grew bits of green thread from their torn edges and stitched themselves together.

Peregrine, still seated, looked at Tassia's hands, which emitted white smoke.

"You understand the ancient magic better than I thought," Peregrine said.

Tassia looked at her knuckles, a sly expression underneath her mask. "One of our weaponsmiths made these, claiming mother of pearl counters witchcraft. Clearly, he was right."

Peregrine chuckled. "Oh, sweetie. I overestimated you, then. If you think I only conjure from one magical property..."

She threw her hand out, causing lily pads and leaves to shake atop the puddle to her right. Yanking her arm skyward, the mucky water rushed vertically. Then pointing at Tassia, the swamp water jetted forward in a whirling funnel.

Tassia didn't retreat, shrieking a battle cry and throwing herself toward it. Twisting mid-air, her lengthy boots – glowing the same molten orange as her blade before – sliced a roundhouse kick through the conjuration. The water burst around her in a puff of mist as she landed.

She faced Peregrine. "I'll ask one final time... what are you supplying Davion with?"

"If you kill me, your answers die here as well," she replied.

Tassia thumbed over her shoulder. "I'll just rummage through your house a bit. I'm sure it's written somewhere."

"Sure, you could try that, but I think my home will crumple you into a little Vampire dumpling," Peregrine replied with a toothy smile.

Tassia clapped her hands together, and the white smoke rising around her knuckles formed into small blades extending from her fists. She pointed one at the Witch. "I'm guessing his ability to live depends on whether you're breathing."

Peregrine tilted her head to one side, crinkly locks of grey and blue hair resting on her shoulder. "I think you'll find destroying this vessel won't bear edible fruit, sweetie."

Tassia glared, eyes squinting in displeasure. She started for her but was immediately cut off as pale roots ensnared her ankles. She sliced them with her claws, but as soon as she removed one, ten more followed. She saw Peregrine raise her arm covered in the vine-like wand overhead, then only darkness.

Peregrine watched as the monstrous plant scarfed Tassia. The outer petals had closed around her and appeared to be chewing her like a child enjoying a sticky treat. Turning away, she waddled back to her home, water and vegetation clearing themselves from her path.

A fist punched through the plant behind her, sounding like an anvil falling on mud. Squishy rips and tears followed. Looking over her shoulder, she saw Tassia stagger out of the remnants, covered in slime.

"Is that your best trick, spinstress?" Tassia said, clenching her fists to make the smoke blades once more.

Peregrine turned on her heel and shot thick ivy for her. Pink flowers sprouted out in wistful puffs as they traveled. Tassia dashed upward a beat to avoid the poisonous-looking foliage, then twisted and shoved off the air towards Peregrine in a weighty cloud of red and silver smoke. More leaves, roots, and branches stabbed at the cagey Vampire, but she dodged or swatted them away. Extending her hand, she could feel the Witch's breath on her knuckles.

"Yaaaah!" Tassia yelped as a wet force slammed into her side, sending her away.

She hit the muddy ground with a hard thump, struggling to breathe as the grimy water held its cylindrical shape and refused to dissipate. Peering through the slits in her mask, she noticed the water was pressing her against the ground, like a guard dog holding a trespasser's ribcage.

"Now, I have a question I'd like answered," Peregrine said.

Tassia looked to one side and saw the Witch standing over her. She continued squirming, trying to break free. When using brute force proved futile, Tassia frantically searched her pouch for another vial of molten sludge.

Peregrine leaned forward, reaching for Tassia's face. "I'd like to see what's behind that mask…"

A glob of heated muck slashed through the water, causing it to evaporate immediately. Peregrine yanked her arm over her face, and a burst of flowers shot from the wand enveloping her arm, soaking up the heated muck and protecting her.

With her adversary distracted, Tassia leaped in Vampiric fashion, appearing like a whirl of colored smoke. As she landed, she sliced a pearlescent smoke-blade through her enemy's arm, cutting the hand free.

"Yraaaaahhh!" Peregrine shriek-snarled in pain, staggering away.

She tensed her arm, trying to grow it back, but Tassia took the opening, pouncing on her prey.

"What are you giving him?" she demanded, clutching the Witch by her throat.

Peregrine grabbed Tassia's hand instinctually to slow the choking. "You can kill this body, but my soul's already spli…"

Tassia shoved a fist through her core, teal blood splattering out. "I'm done with conversation."

Releasing Peregrine's neck, she let the Witch fall onto a limestone slab. The body landed with a meaty crunch, like the sound of chopping wet wood.

"Now let's see what secrets you hold," Tassia stated through gritted teeth, turning back and stomping towards Peregrine's home.

As she approached it, Tassia noticed the lights inside slowly dimming. A sign the spell empowering it earlier was dying. Suddenly, she was knocked back as the roof exploded from its perch. Raging flame gushed overhead in a rush of towering heat.

She groaned at the sharp pain shooting across her back, having fallen on a limestone slab. Coughing, she felt the sting in her ribs as she recovered from having the wind knocked out of her. Gasping a few times, she held her side and reached into another pouch for a vial of blood with her free hand. Having sucked its contents to restore her vitality, she sighed in relief as her pain disappeared, along with her fatigue from the previous battle.

"You can destroy your evidence, Witch, but I have one more place to visit in this swamp. And I have a feeling it houses similar answers," she cursed, climbing back to her feet.

After collecting herself, she stomped off in the direction of Davion's cabin, leaving the magical corpse and burning cottage in her wake.

CHAPTER
<u>SIXTEEN</u>

HE STEPPED OVER the dead man, nonchalantly heading for the remote cabin. It sat just a stone's throw away from where a large river met one of the Intercontinent's edge oceans. The magical bodies of water ran off one side, then underneath the floating nation, to finally emerge at another point.

A second corpse met his feet after passing the threshold of his master's cabin. Around the corner, he heard crackling and slurping, telltale signs a bloodthirst was being quenched. Rounding a logwood wall, he found Geldam Viruticus sitting in a thin chair, fangs shoved deep into the carotid of a glassy-eyed victim. Geldam's eyes met Davion's, but he didn't release his mandible's grip. Davion stood silently, waiting to be spoken to rather than interrupting him.

Geldam finally let go of the man, whose green eyes turned grey, showing all semblance of life had been sucked free. His victim's head smacked against the wood floor after being carelessly dropped.

"You have something to share?" Geldam asked gruffly.

Davion gave a curt nod. "My suspicions lead me…"

Geldam waved off his subordinate, abruptly leaving his chair and turning away. "Suspicions don't give me justice."

Davion inhaled deeply, stopping himself from chasing approval by replying too quickly. He had to appear confident and in control. Badgering the Count with his reasons would only push Geldam to disregard them.

Once the silence became too uncomfortable, Geldam broke it. "Out with it then."

Davion stepped forward and took a seat. Geldam glanced over his shoulder and saw him take a long pull of raspberry blood-wine directly from the bottle.

"It's been that kind of week for you as well?" Geldam asked, noting his guest's exhausted demeanor.

"The travel is tiring, but it's nothing compared to your grief, Sir," he answered, setting the bottle down.

Geldam stared out a foggy window towards the river and sighed. "Does it ever get better, Davion?"

"Why do you ask, Sir?" he replied.

"Many Snared to our kind turn those close to them. They'll arrive in Vèspige looking to join a House with a loved one or friend in tow. You were alone when you joined our House, so I'm assuming you've experienced loss before…"

Davion slowly turned the bottle in his fingers absentmindedly. "Your assumptions are correct; I've experienced loss before my time in the Court. Regarding if it gets better… it doesn't."

Geldam grunted and didn't answer, continuing to stare out the window.

155

Davion shook his head. "But it doesn't get worse. It just becomes different. You'll have two selves, one with them and one without." As he finished, he took another drink.

He found it odd to give advice about grief to one of the entities partly responsible for his own personal suffering.

Geldam opened a cupboard and rummaged about, eventually retrieving another bottle. "So, tell me what you've learned," he said before taking a swig.

"Do you have any knowledge of Countess Fiona's arrival to the Court or the origin of her Snare?" Davion asked.

Geldam cocked an eye at him. "You know it's uncouth to ask about a Vampire's beginnings."

Davion rested his forearms on the table, interlacing his fingers. "I know it's inappropriate to inquire, but considering the circumstances, I had to ask."

Geldam finished another sip, rolling the wine in his mouth a bit before sucking it back through his fangs. "I've not the faintest clue how she joined our kind. I figured you'd know more than me, considering you'd spent so much time with Adelina."

Davion shrugged. "We avoided sharing too much. And unfortunately, any opportunity I had seems lost at this point. Now that I'm in an investigatory capacity, she's more interested in prying about how our House is doing and more guarded about anything related to her own."

Geldam pursed his lips. "Well, I hope you have more to offer than questions, Davion. The idea this killer works for one of our own has everyone fortifying their ranks and relationships. If you don't find answers that we can bring to the Counts, the other Houses will create their own."

Davion took another deep swig from his bottle, then sighed in relief. Surveying the label, he nodded in satisfaction at its dry yet fruity flavor, making a mental note of the vintage so he'd remember to drink it again before leaving Vèspige.

"I do have some compelling information about Fiona and why I believe she was complicit in working with Carneth. The trail also leads back to her assisting Malnuvious with his treachery. But for her to admit that in front of everyone at the next meeting, I'll need your help."

He heard an odd sound upstairs and perked an ear. He'd already been visited by Davion this week and hadn't expected him back so soon. He walked the five steps it took to cross his cell, approaching several shelves bolted to the stone wall. Surveying his week's food supply, he snagged a pear and took a hearty bite.

Then a thought crossed his mind. *'It might not be Davion...'*

The door down the hallway creaked open, followed by light footsteps along the stone floor. Carneth slunk to a shadowy corner, quickly checking his pockets to ensure he had every necessary item.

Laughter from a feminine voice greeted him. "This is where he's hiding you."

"Have you come to free me?" Carneth asked, playing into the lie that he had been captured.

Tassia tilted her head, face covered by her mask and shrouded in her hood. "That's one way to view it..."

Carneth steeled himself, reaching into his pocket for a smoke bomb. "So, you're here to suck my veins dry then?"

"I'm just here to move you to your new cell," she answered, dangling a key ring from one finger.

He watched her unlock the door anxiously. "When does Fiona help me like she promised?" he lied, trying every hand given to him.

Tassia laughed. "Did Davion give you that little crumb? I knew he planned to lay blame at our House's feet."

She swung the gate open with one hand and was immediately met with a burst of smoke and sparks. Reflexively, she leaped backward, giving Carneth the opening to dart from the cell and race for his sword. His outstretched hand felt the powerful blade's magic lap at his fingertips; then, she was upon him.

His eyes bulged in their sockets at the suffocating surge of pain enveloping his throat.

"Don't worry. I promise we'll keep you alive," she said with a sharp, menacing laugh.

Feeling himself being lifted, he kicked his feet in futility, clawing at her grasp around his neck.

"Until you're no longer useful," she finished with a wry smile across her lips.

He struggled tenaciously against the chokehold despite darkness devouring his eyesight and the growing tingle of numbness. He fought until inky-black nothingness swallowed his senses and vision entirely.

CHAPTER
SEVENTEEN

STONE GARGOYLES WITH bat faces were perched atop two ebony pillars at the entrance to Elbourne Manor.

'I wouldn't be surprised if they had the magic to bring those things to life,' Davion thought uneasily, staring out his window.

It was the oldest and most formal castle in the Court. After their carriage passed the gates, Davion noticed a few groundskeepers tending to several hedges with red and yellow foliage. Most of the other manors had moved on from the classic taste of living landscaping, opting to add more stonework sculptures and fountains instead. Since Vampires were nocturnal, plant life didn't have the same vibrance as carved marble in moonlight. The Elbournes felt themselves beyond maintaining the ever-changing fashion standards. Their castle was a grouping of tall towers of varying sizes with spiked steeples. Sharp, venomous, vicious. It looked like a forest of upright razors ready to stab the night sky.

Davion walked alongside Geldam through the tall arched double doors. Nothing had changed inside the manor since he first joined the Court, but it was still impressive. The curved forty-foot ceilings, intricately carved columns, and painted portraits of every ranking Royal along the walls caught his eye. As they headed for the throne room, Davion tried to hide the heavy lump of unease welling in his throat. The estate's powerful structure, haunting magnificence, and deadly beauty made him feel like a rodent being led through the den of a serpent.

Davion eyed the inhabitants as they entered, checking for anyone missing. The only House not represented was Fiona's. The attendees were uncomfortably mingling, biding time until everyone arrived. Of course, he couldn't mingle with anyone until after the meeting was adjourned. Doing so would leave him open to scrutiny about his impartiality.

'Lucky for me, the only House I keep being seen with is Mayjere. The only one I plan to implicate at the moment,' he mused, smiling.

Through the corner of his eye, he caught a woman wearing a red trumpet gown with a billowing section of black and white lace below her knee.

'I hope you enjoy this grandeur while it lasts,' he muttered under his breath.

Baron and Baroness Elbourne approached the raised platform where their thrones sat. The Baron lifted a slender arm, and everyone fell silent.

"Davion will open tonight's session. Please find a seat," he said before gesturing towards the cluster of chairs a foot behind the group of attendees.

"Thank you, Baron," Davion responded graciously, "Before I speak, I'd like to open the floor to anyone who has information of their own."

Concerned expressions crossed the majority of seated Counts. Davion wanted to put them on their heels, simmer their tensions and reservations of each other to the surface. While most Houses were clean of any crimes, they were still used to their peaceful bliss and loathed the idea of being scrutinized. They'd be eager to pile onto his claims once he accused Fiona, looking for any opportunity to snatch innocence for themselves and end the investigation. If she wasn't behind the Wayward trap, he knew she'd at least share why she knew details about the potion no one else did.

'If she learned that fact from another Count, she'll reveal their name once she's backed into a corner,' Davion thought.

Only the sounds of a few anxious coughs and shuffling seats serenaded the room's silence.

'Good,' Davion told himself.

He wanted undivided control of the conversation before starting the meeting. "I understand why you'd all be so reserved. However…"

Fiona rose from her seat. "I have something to offer."

Davion held his breath as she briskly made her way to his side. He noticed two small envelopes in her hands.

She handed them to him. "I'm concerned about your impartiality during this affair. I want to know why you've been constantly corresponding with Peregrine and Yaspen well before this gathering."

161

Davion held the letters, stunned at being confronted about his secret alliances. He continued gawking at them, unable to respond.

"You can turn them over and inspect them. The seals are still intact," she continued.

Davion flipped them over and verified her claims.

He looked over at her. "I've been tasked with investigating these crimes. Isn't it obvious that I would tap two incredibly connected people?"

She raised an eyebrow, pointing a lengthy claw – painted in white – at the envelopes. "Those are dated before you were given that title by the Baron and Baroness."

"They were also helpful in locating Carneth," he retorted, glaring at her.

She bowed her head facetiously. "My apologies. I can understand that."

Davion turned to address the crowd and move the conversation forward, but Fiona quickly lifted a finger, interrupting him. "Although, I would like to ask if the rest of us may be privy to the contents. If they contain information concerning Carneth – sent well before you were given rule over his fate – I think it best we all know. It would make it easier to assist you with your work."

He licked a fang nervously, unsure how to best respond.

She continued. "I was given those by Tassia. I offered her services to Geldam, hoping she could help you catch Carneth. During her travels, she saw one of Yaspen's messengers left for dead on the side of the road – mauled by a ghoul," she shook her head, "The rest of his effects are en route to Yaspen now," she finished in a solemn tone.

Davion – wanting to retake command of the meeting – ripped the letter from Yaspen open and read it aloud.

Davion,

There is one bit of information I didn't share with you in person earlier. I have in my possession one of the Hunting Masks Carneth stole. Since Countess Fiona rules over that section of the Court, I felt it best I reach out to her first. I have it safely locked away until it can be returned. I plan on delivering it to the Baron and Baroness - hopefully by proxy through her - as I am not allowed in their presence after banishment. If she is unwilling, I'd ask that you see if Count Geldam would oblige my request.

Sincerely,
Yaspen

His gamble paid off. Remembering that Yaspen mentioned a letter about the Mask when they last met, he hoped the contents would be something non-incriminating. However, the letter from Peregrine was another matter entirely. Its unknown contents truly concerned him.

He slammed the letter down on the small round table in front of the Counts. "I'm not afraid to disclose relevant correspondence when it's beneficial for all of you to know," he said, hoping his overt gesture would deflect any further inquiries. Looking to favorably tilt the verbal scales, he turned to Fiona. "I find it hard to believe, however, that someone as volatile as Tassia just happened to pass by the right messenger at the right time."

She sighed, placing her hands together gently. "I only share what she relayed to me. The seals were not broken, and I brought them directly to you. I have nothing to h…"

163

"Only at the most favorable time for you," he argued.

She crossed an arm over her waist, resting her elbow in it while placing a finger on her chin. "And why would this be advantageous to me, Davion? After coming to my home and asking about the Wayward plot, I only felt I should ensure there be witnesses when delivering something like this."

Count Geldam abruptly stood upright, knocking his chair over. "What Wayward plot?! Davion, you never mentioned that to me," he lied.

Davion looked to his superior, who barely squinted one eyelid in return. Showing that he trusted Davion while playing ignorant to loft up an opportunity for him. The beginnings of their plan to further pin Fiona down.

Davion seized the moment. "I came to her with questions about their plot because it's likely connected to whichever House orchestrated Carneth's attacks. When I spoke with you about it, you mentioned details of their potion I'd never heard before," he shifted his whole body and faced her directly, "tell me the truth, Countess. Was House Mayjere working in concert with House Malnuvious to steal the throne all those years ago?!"

Agitated, murmurous chatter overtook the small crowd. Davion – arms clasped behind his back – stood confidently, waiting for her rebuttal. None came. A sour expression of contempt was her only reply.

As the whispers amplified to full-on arguing, Baron Elbourne stood. "Silence!" he commanded.

Quiet immediately followed.

"Your claims are concerning, Davion," he said, descending the two steps of his raised throne platform, "I

164

understand your fervor in resolving this, but I cannot allow our Court to be shredded from within. Before we move any further with this, I wish to speak with Carneth myself."

Davion swallowed fearfully; he'd accounted for many contingencies when planning his courtroom chess game. However, he hadn't thought that – upon taking the lead – Baron Elbourne would simply flip the board off the table.

He needed to stall enough to weave a new web. "I can gather my supplies and be ready to take you there tomorrow n…"

Baron Elbourne waved him off, gliding towards the door. "You will take me there tonight, Davion."

His boots shlepped through the mud as he led Baron Elbourne to his hideout. He'd graciously been offered the chance to plead his case to the Baron during their carriage ride. It was hard to tell whether the Vampire ruler was intrigued by Davion's logic or simply humoring him to alleviate the boredom of travel.

'He asked Yaspen about the Waywards, looking for one of them,' Davion had told him earlier, *'I think that whichever House hired him also assisted House Malnuvious with their treachery,'* he'd concluded.

Baron Elbourne had studied Davion. Peering eerily into his eyes. Although Davion had felt nothing, he was worried that he was possibly succumbing to another secret spell from the ancient Vampire. He knew their kind could mesmerize humans who let their emotional guard down. Could someone as powerful as the Baron take it one step further? He'd heard rumors during his time as a Wayward that Vampires once possessed the capability to unveil glimpses of people's past actions – just by catching their sight.

'*No. Those are merely overstated legends,*' he thought, '*if he could see those things, he'd have already carved me to bits rather than trudge across this muck.*'

Of course, only Davion had to actually walk through it. His unexpected companion floated elegantly the entire way.

"He's downstairs, Baron," Davion instructed while leading him to the set of stairs leading to the cell below the cabin.

Davion lit the flame of a small lantern just past the entrance. While Vampires had night vision, the gesture was a cordial one. Courtly culture dictated that not lighting a path for a guest insinuated they weren't worthy of the effort.

Turning from the wall-mounted sconce, Davion's stomach dropped. If he'd had a pulse, it would have stopped completely.

"I expected more of your ability to secure the prisoner," Baron Elbourne stated coldly.

After inspecting the empty cell, he turned to Davion, his words spoken in a chillingly calm tone. "You have until our next meeting to bring him to me, or I will eviscerate you and your entire House."

CHAPTER EIGHTEEN

CARNETH FELT as if a hammer was captured inside his skull and currently mounting an escape by thumping the interior of it. Blinking feverishly, he hoped to steady the throbbing pain and regain his vision.

"Food is on the table," a deep voice said.

Carneth glanced one way, then another, before spotting a table with a bowl and metal spoon. Crawling to it, he noticed something weighing down his ankle.

'Bastard chained me down,' he muttered after observing the cast iron clamp around it.

It gave him enough room to reach the table but not enough to reach anything else of worth. He took a spoonful of the oatmeal and ate it with trepidation.

'Not bad for prison gruel,' he thought, taking another bite.

Observing his quarters, he saw his chain ran to the back of a cave. Flat grey dirt beneath him, jagged stone surrounding him. Unfortunately, he couldn't tell how deep they were or what might lie beyond their location since the tunnel at the entrance made a sharp turn just a few feet outside.

Surveying the walls, he understood why they were hidden in such remote quarters. Hunting Masks lined many shelves along an entire wall to one side, while potions and unique trinkets covered the opposite one.

Several yards from him, a looming figure pounded something with a thin pickaxe. The creature had the tall, hulking figure of a troll, but instead of a troll's usual stringy hair, sickly toned skin, and tattered clothing, it wore a patterned tunic, had thick black locks pulled into a braid, and ebony skin with a polished sheen. It paid no attention to him, continuing its work instead.

Having regained his wit, he decided to interact with his captor. "How long until our master returns?" he inquired.

"She usually comes every week," it answered flatly, tiny sparks flying from the object it was hammering.

Carneth stood, trying to peer closer at what the creature was crafting. "Is that another Mask?"

The behemoth looked over his shoulder at him. "Why so many questions? You are a prisoner here, like me. We are here to serve, not question."

Carneth crossed his arms. "Serve? I can't imagine someone of your stature being held against their will…" touching a finger to his chin and pondering for a moment, "well, anywhere."

It faced him, frowning. Not in anger at his proposition but rather in contemplation. "When one completes the prayer, I am required to come… if I'm not already serving."

As it turned away to continue hammering, Carneth stepped forward to question further, then felt the chain roughly yank his ankle. He yowled in anguish and flipped the table over, spilling the last few bites of oats from the bowl. Hearing the clanging, the creature whipped its head around.

"Did you destroy my creation?" it asked.

Carneth pointed towards the mess. "You're talking about the food?"

Three lumbering steps followed, and Carneth scrambled away, back against a wall.

"Most wait until I cannot see them do so," its booming voice said, towering over him.

"I...I only did so in frustration," Carneth stammered before giving a meek shrug, hoping his submissive posture would gain him some shred of clemency.

It squinted, observing him. "You are an odd one. Your name, fellow prisoner?"

"C...Carneth," he finally got out.

It nodded and stood upright before taking the few steps back to its workbench.

"Will you be in servitude forever?" Carneth asked, slowly creeping back to the table and carefully repositioning it upright.

It didn't answer, continuing to hammer instead.

Carneth cleaned up what he could of the remaining mess before returning to his seat. Despite its size and presence, the creature possibly had a friendly character underneath.

'It could kill me with a flick of its finger, but if I just wait here silently, I can't imagine that Vampire assassin lets me live either.' he thought.

He decided to take his chances. "Since we're in the same predicament, I thought we should get to know one another..."

The creature froze, straightening its posture. "You gave your name, so I can share some of mine. You may know me as El-Kazir, Wrathfire, or Ahman Rael."

Carneth – standing with crossed arms – bit his lower lip, squinted, and shrugged. "Those names are unfamiliar to me..."

The creature's black eyes narrowed.

"But they sound exceptional," Carneth interjected, "I think I'll go with..." giving a solitary wave of one finger, "Ahman Rael."

"Tassia commanded I create these," Ahman said, slowly gesturing at the many works on the wall. He then pointed at Carneth, "but she has given you no task. The Spirits..." it trailed off, placing a hefty palm against its head, desperate to find the thought.

Carneth's brow furrowed. "Does she have a spell over you, Ahman?"

It shook its head. "When brought to this mortal realm, I lost... a piece of myself. Usually, I am called to bring someone to the higher plane. Whoever initially called me here has not returned in years..."

Carneth scratched his chin for several minutes while his cellmate gathered itself. *'I haven't heard of magic that calls someone to Moncroix, but stranger tales have been told about our Intercontinent.'*

It blinked once and then stood straight again. "Tassia took their place. I am here to serve her until I am called by another prayer."

170

"Any chance you'd be willing to answer my prayer and break this little chain here with that hammer?" Carneth asked with a coy smile.

Ahman stared blankly at his sarcasm.

"Not one for playful banter, eh?" Carneth mused aloud.

"I am commanded to create... and to keep you here," Ahman stated.

Carneth exhaled sharply. "Well, hopefully, someone prays for El-Kazoo..."

"El-Kazir," Ahman interrupted.

"Yes, of course... El-Kazir. Hopefully, that prayer comes through before next week," he finished.

Carneth reached for his hip and felt the one option he had left still strapped to himself. *Thankfully, she didn't notice that,'* he thought, *'Now, hopefully, it's enough to reach my blade this time,'* he noted, staring across the room at his sword, which rested on a shelf near Ahman Rael.

CHAPTER NINETEEN

FEAR SLITHERED AND coiled inside his stomach like a snake through grass. Sweeping across the sky from branch to branch, Davion silently prayed between anxious breaths. He knew it was more than a coincidence that Carneth happened to be missing from his cell after being confronted by Fiona about his letters.

'I fear my prayers to Varkin may be too late,' he thought, leaping down to the marshy floor.

He swallowed down his anxiety, hoping his calls to the Spirit of power would be answered. Of course, the Spirit's visits to the mortal realm were incredibly rare. Outside of Celiss – the Wayward leader that Snared him – he didn't know of anyone who could connect with them at will.

'And that only allowed Celiss to give meager magical enhancements,' he pondered.

Anyone visited directly by one of the Spirits received their gifts through a chance encounter or by employing the correct combination of magic and prayer. Vampires and Wolven tribes were the exceptions since they could apply specific bites that converted a mere mortal into one of their own. Whether that was a blessing or curse hadn't been unanimously agreed upon.

'I know I'd never damn anyone to this purgatory,' Davion told himself, running across the moss.

If Fiona, or even worse, Tassia, had visited Peregrine before him, he feared what might be revealed.

'Hopefully, she holds her tongue,' Davion said to himself.

Witches were fickle beings. Most held secrets until their last breath, but a scant few divulged anything for the right sum. Deep down, he believed Peregrine fit in the former column. After years of visiting her remote cottage, he truly regarded her as a friend.

Rounding a set of trees leading to the clearing in front of her home, he slowed his run to a brisk walk. His eyes searched every direction, he didn't notice anyone present. His Vampire shriek a mile earlier hadn't yielded results either. Squinting, he noticed something a few yards from her front porch.

"Oh no…" Davion exhaled, wide-eyed.

Approaching the slumped figure in the weeds, his fears became fact.

Peregrine was dead.

Her carcass lay on its side, blood oozing from a gaping wound between her chest and stomach. Vines grew around her desecrated figure. He knelt down and slowly reached a finger toward her. Thin spikes shot up from the vines, causing him to retract his hand.

"It's as if those damn things intended to bite me!" he exclaimed.

Teal light – the same color as her blood – seeped out from the vine's underside.

"Either this swamp intends to eat her, or Peregrine's magic is beyond anyone's knowledge," Davion noted. Disconcerted, he climbed to his feet.

It still felt unbelievable. How could she be gone? He'd only just spoken with her a few days prior. His mind raced through scenarios of what he could have done. How he could have dealt with whatever threat she faced. The sting of her death was different from the mourning he suffered after losing his brethren. Reaching deeper into his soul, he discovered why. It was more than her friendship. She was the last link between himself and the Waywards. With this tie severed, nothing remained of his former self. He'd lost them forever. Nothing remained of his former life.

"I thought I could only lose them once," he muttered aloud, "I guess... I was wrong," he finished, tears welling under his eyes.

He shook his head fiercely and blinked them away. There was no time for pity or sadness. He'd exhausted every ounce of that as the melancholy messenger of House Viruticus.

"This is the end," he told himself, "I have nothing left to sacrifice to this Court."

He interlaced his fingers with his index ones pointed, touching them to his forehead. Making a final prayer to the Spirit of death to safely guard her soul in the afterlife. Sighing deeply, he slowly lowered his hands. Knowing it was his last moment with her, he exaggerated every gesture, not wanting his time with her to end. Taking another deep breath, he mustered the emotional fortitude to leave her side. With each step, his heart tugged at his chest. Yearning for him to turn back and not let her go. But he couldn't grieve any longer. He had to find Carneth.

"Maybe I'll find a sign among this wreckage," he wondered aloud.

Stepping inside the charred remains of her residence, Davion noticed something glowing dimly near one of the windows. Stooping down, he picked it up and inspected what appeared to be a chunk of painted wood the size of a medallion. Mist billowed lightly from the edges.

"What have we here..." he said, noticing how familiar the lines of paint were, "Of course, this would be the only thing to survive a fire," he said, smirking.

"Once I find Carneth, there's no answer you can give that will prove your innocence," Davion declared while stuffing the piece of Tassia's Hunting Mask into his pocket.

"Never thought I'd have a reason to come here again," Yaspen told his carriage driver.

Peering through the upper reaches of his window, he stared at the looming spires of Elbourne Manor slicing the sky before him. Fortunately, the winter clouds withheld their rain this evening. The driver opened his door for him, and Yaspen stepped out, carefully holding his hat in place with one hand.

He inhaled, then let out a heavy sigh. "Not a single crumb of this gawdy estate has changed since I came here for sentencing."

Another person stepped out from the large carriage and joined him.

"Are you worried, Yaspen?" the stout, bearded man asked.

Yaspen shook his head. "Quite the opposite. This Court has done all it can to me. I've got nothing to fear from these parasites."

Looking to one side, he saw Fiona approaching.

"Who's this one?" she asked with a curt upward nod.

"He's a friend I've entrusted with the custody of such a precious item," Yaspen replied, thumbing toward the wood box in the burly man's hands.

"He looks like protection for you, rather than the mask," she noted.

Yaspen sputtered a quick laugh. "Countess Fiona... intimidated? I'm shocked at the prospect."

She raised an eyebrow, ignoring his comment. "Does this one have a name?"

The man tucked the box under one arm and extended his hand. "I'm Thavin."

Arms still crossed, she sneered at the gesture. "I take it – Thavin – that based on your rustic attire and unkempt hair, you hail from the Eastern Mountains."

Glancing at his hand, he shrugged off the snub and shifted the box back into both arms. "Raised in Low Slope. A village at the base of Mount Sealth."

"Low Slope, eh..." she replied snidely, looking down her nose while holding her chin.

"He's one of us," Yaspen interjected, "Not sure how he was turned, but after it happened, he fled his village. Fearful of what he might do. I recruited him since living in Vèspige probably wouldn't suit his tastes."

Fiona smiled. "Don't mistake my expression for belittlement, Yaspen. If I'm to allow you..." she then jutted her chin once towards Thavin, "and Mr. Low Slope inside. Then I must vet you both first."

Yaspen smiled and tipped the brim of his hat. "Are we vetted sufficiently?"

She smiled wryly. "For now..."

Turning on her heel. She motioned for them to follow her inside.

"Baron and Baroness, I sponsor the visit of this banished one," she said, bowing graciously.

Baron Elbourne stood from his throne, glaring at Yaspen and Thavin. Yaspen knelt on one knee, elbowing Thavin so he'd follow suit.

"May I speak, or shall I speak through her, Baron?" Yaspen asked, head stooped.

Baron Elbourne didn't answer, continuing to scowl disdainfully.

The Baroness raised a slender hand. "You may speak through her only, unless we address you directly, banished one."

Fiona turned and held her hands out before Thavin, who looked to Yaspen for confirmation, then set the box in them.

She faced the two rulers, resting on their thrones. "This is one of the Hunting Masks, turned over to Yaspen by Carneth himself. He wanted me to inspect it, but due to his..." she looked over her shoulder at him, "current status with the Court, he decided it best to have it presented to you directly."

She bowed customarily, then strode forward and handed the small crate over to the Vampire rulers.

Baron Elbourne set it on an end table next to his throne, then stuck out his hand. "The key?"

Fiona looked to Yaspen, who removed a small gold key from his pocket, along with a thin vial of potion.

"Tell him to pour this over the lock first," he instructed her under his breath.

She nodded and then brought the items forward. Baron Elbourne regarded the potion, then looked at Fiona. She understood that going through such motions for a banished Vampire was beneath him. Hurriedly completing the task, she opened the now unlocked lid for him. He shooed her aside before reaching inside it.

Retrieving the Mask, he took it to a shadowy section near a tall pillar. Keeping it away from the flickering flames atop the sconces adorning his walls. The darkness brought out the Vampiric night vision inherent to his eyes. After turning it back and forth a few times, he tossed it aside.

Rushing forward in a whirling gust of red robes, Baron Elbourne stood face to face with Yaspen. "Is what you brought here truly from that killer?!" he inquired harshly.

Despite the other two ducking away, Yaspen stood solidly in place. In his mind, he had nothing to fear. The Mask had come from Carneth, and he wanted Baron Elbourne to see the truth in his posture as well as his words.

He raised his chin confidently. "Now you see why I had to bring it before you directly."

Baron Elbourne held his position, inches from Yaspen, his red eyes staring intently into the banished one's.

Countess Fiona slowly retook her footing and scooped the mask from the floor, hoping she'd find what had upset her ruler.

"You brought a fake here?!" she yelled in shock.

Baroness Elbourne joined Fiona, looking for herself.

Yaspen continued. "When I initially saw it under normal candlelight, I was as fooled as you all were. However, when I inspected it further in darkness…"

Countess Fiona whirled towards him. "Don't lie to us, Yaspen! You think we're foolish enough to fall for such a farce…"

"He's not lying," Baron Elbourne interrupted, having read Yaspen's eyes.

She stood still, inhaling deeply to stave off her rage at the situation.

"Three of our own were killed by Carneth," Baroness Elbourne said while gliding forward, her white and gold robes fluttering as she traveled, "We know Geldam has Thadric's mask…" she stated before looking at Fiona inquisitively, "and Davion returned the one he took when capturing Carneth."

Fiona nodded.

The Baroness pointed at Yaspen. "Then who has the third?"

Yaspen lowered his chin, tipping his hat respectfully. "I believe that's a question for Carneth…"

CHAPTER
TWENTY

CARNETH TOUCHED A hand to his hip, finding it odd how the Hunting Mask had morphed itself to snugly fit around the curve of his leg. It hadn't broken its position or slipped from its spot since he hid it there. When meeting Yaspen, he'd wondered how long it would be before the merchant discovered that he'd received a fraudulent one.

'*Hopefully, he understood my predicament. Having every Vampire after my hide required me to equip every tool I could find. Or, at the very least, he'll respect the gamesmanship,*' he mused with a smile.

The Vampire merchant reflected a cunning personality that would appreciate Carneth's ploy. Thankfully, he'd held onto the fact that he secretly carried a mask from everyone, including Davion. He needed an ace up his sleeve should the situation arise. This stone prison seemed like the perfect fit to play that card. Before he could utilize it, however, he had to uncover more about Ahman Rael, The last thing he needed was for the immense creature to squash him. The ten-foot-tall muscular man-shaped behemoth seemed easily capable of doing so.

"Tell me, Ahman..." Carneth began, using only the first half of the name. Which it didn't seem to mind. "You mentioned answering another prayer – and whoever called you here being gone now – so, why are you stuck then?"

Ahman glanced up from the mask he was bending into shape. "She assumed the role of that believer when she found me and spoke my truth."

Carneth slowly chewed through the lump of oatmeal before replying. "What would it take for her prayer to be countered?"

"She must perish," Ahman answered flatly before returning to his work.

Carneth raised his eyebrows. "Till death do you part, eh?"

Eating another spoonful, he stared at the peculiar being. At first, he'd believed his cellmate to be nothing more than a golem, created from inanimate material to serve Fiona, who sent her subordinate Tassia to deliver instructions. But Ahman was far more sophisticated than the statuesque slaves, often brought to life by Warlocks. He'd learned that from their conversations and watching it craft the many masks and potions lining the walls.

'No...' thought Carneth, 'a Golem could punch an enemy or haul heavy lumber but not expertly construct such intricate items.'

"Why did the potions fail?" Carneth asked.

Ahman's eyes narrowed. "They did not fail."

Carneth squinted. "Fiona wanted you to make something that hid her Snare. According to what I've heard from our chats – and ones with a few others regarding the matter – their effects didn't last long enough to be valuable to her," he said, holding his spoon aloft and gesturing while he spoke as if conducting his words.

"Their effective duration does not mean they failed," the booming voice answered.

Carneth leaned forward, pointing his spoon at Ahman. "You've sold me this line that you're a fallen god. So, what's stopping it from being more effective?"

Ahman set the mask down, sitting upright and staring intently at Carneth. Rising from its seat, it walked over to a shelf and retrieved one of the vials, along with a metal bowl. Carneth held his breath and readied himself in case Ahman finally turned on him.

'If I time offending him right, maybe he'll swing and miss, breaking this pesky chain,' he told himself.

But Ahman played with the potion instead, pouring it into the bowl and sprinkling a few powders on top before stirring it with a thin metal rod. After mixing the concoction, he shook the rod once, then dipped it back into the elixir.

"The magic of these Spirits cannot be overridden by mine," Ahman said, lifting a bundle of tangled red lines with the rod.

"Is that a Vampire Snare?" Carneth asked, leaning forward to get a better view.

Ahman shrugged. "The best foundation of one I could make."

Carneth held his chin for a moment, thinking over his words carefully. "Is that why it's more effective with Snared humans?"

"What do you mean..." Ahman inquired.

"The potion is less effective on someone fully enhanced with the Spirit's magic, like a Vampire. But a human…" Carneth tilted his head in thought while pointing at Ahman, "seems able to accept your imposter Snare for longer."

Carneth shook his head, eyes wide. "Just when I believe I've seen all the magic this Intercontinent has to offer. If the other nations knew the spoils beyond Qulàire's wall," he placed his chin in his palm, "but most of them don't even believe Vampires exist."

Ahman raised a brow. "Why wouldn't they?"

"It's complicated, but the best way I could summarize it is to say that anyone visiting Moncroix never reaches the Midland. They won't allow it. You must be native to this Intercontinent to be allowed passage here," Carneth explained.

"How would they know if one was born here or beyond? Many humans have similar appearances?" Ahman asked.

Carneth threw up his hands. "I don't understand the inner workings of every facet within Moncroix."

Ahman smiled, bowing his head slightly. "Now you seem to understand."

Carneth crossed his arms. "It's different than a supposed fallen god who can't tell me how he bakes his cookies…"

"Is that how you perceive my work?" it answered in a low tone.

He gave a deep sigh and then waved a hand toward the wall of masks. "You're making everything here from scratch using your own recipes. That's different than expecting me to know everything about a vast city I was only a small part of."

Ahman looked to one side, contemplating his response before returning his gaze to Carneth. "You bother me with

183

questions. Now I annoy you with some of mine. I don't see the difference."

Carneth grunted as Ahman laughed in his booming baritone.

"Definitely not a golem," Carneth muttered.

He rested his cheek on his fist, bored, believing he'd exhausted every question Ahman was capable of answering. Then another thought came to him.

"Why don't you know more about Moncroix? Didn't you claim to be a god of creation…"

"Foundation," Ahman interrupted.

"Yes, that one. Well, if you're actually a foundation god, wouldn't you know this place a little better?" Carneth finished incredulously.

"I was not responsible for the foundation of this place. The Spirits you call to were. It's unfortunate they don't seem to be whole anymore. They're splintering caused this magi…" Ahman trailed off, grabbing at his head again. His face a mixture of pain and confusion.

'Happens every time he speaks about the Spirits at length,' Carneth noted, rising from his seat.

Ahman turned away from him, then knelt down and braced a palm on the floor, recovering from the impromptu migraine. Carneth observed him while slinking over to the location where his chain was bolted to the floor. Placing himself close to its secured position left him enough slack for his next move. He'd spoken with the supposed god enough to understand a possible weakness.

'Maybe that's part of how she imprisons him,' Carneth pondered, reaching for the mask on his hip.

'If this thing can project a monster from thought, I hope it can conjure up what I'm imagining,' he plotted, closing his eyes while taking a moment to envision the most terrorizing visualization of the Spirit of Death. *'If that image I was taught as a child mirrors a glimpse of reality, this might work.'*

He yanked the mask free, quickly placing it over his face.

"You speak of us again?!" he asked in a commanding tone.

Ahman whipped his head towards Carneth.

"I knew you were more than another prisoner!" Ahman answered defiantly.

"She has no use for you. As the superior gods, we will fulfill her prayers now," Carneth continued, the Mask altering the pitch of his voice to a creaky howl.

Ahman stomped towards Carneth.

Carneth lept aside as a huge fist swung downward, breaking his chain.

"Thanks," Carneth said under his breath, snatching a pack from the floor.

Ahman spun towards Carneth, who continued projecting the image of a skeleton topped with curling horns, clothed in fur armor, and drenched in lime green flames.

"You'll remain trapped here forever, Ahman Rael!" Carneth proclaimed, holding his sword aloft and activating its flames.

Ahman's posture stiffened, unsure how to react.

Carneth whirled on his heel and cackled, running through the translucent gold curtain of light blanketing the room's entrance.

"I hope her seal holds true," he said between pants.

He'd run for several yards and, after not hearing any pursuing footsteps, assumed Fiona's magic veil over the doorway worked. Looking ahead with his sword's flamelight, he noticed a small cutout to his left and a long tunnel to his right. He crept towards the circular room at his left, deciding to inspect it before taking the long tunnel, which was likely an exit.

"There's plenty here worth taking," Carneth said, a wry smile crossing one corner of his mouth.

He seized several hunting masks and potions from a shelf, stuffing them into the pack he'd stolen earlier. After snatching as many wares as the pack would hold from Fiona's stash, he left the small room and took the tunnel. Trudging uphill for what seemed like a mile, faint moonlight eventually greeted him.

Standing in the field of tall tan grass beyond the cave's entrance, he could see curling waves from one of Moncroix's edge oceans. Hearing their rhythmic slamming against the muddy beach calmed his nerves. He closed his eyes and smiled, letting the wind whip through his hair while inhaling the scent of saltwater. Relishing that pure moment of escape from captivity. Eventually opening them, he removed the hunting mask and glanced back at the mouth of the cave.

"I'll miss our conversations, Ahman," he said with a chuckle, "If everything goes to plan, you won't be serving Fiona much longer."

Steeling himself, Carneth turned from the water and strode into the faintly lit forest. He needed to find Davion and couldn't spare a second.

CHAPTER
TWENTY-ONE

"THIS RUM HAS a nice bite to it," Yaspen noted, swirling his short glass crafted with the finest crystal.

His riding companion took a swig, then investigated his own cup. "It's a bit mild," Thavin replied.

Yaspen laughed lightly. "You Wolven have such enhanced sense of smell, but your taste," he took another sip, "is severely lacking."

Thavin shrugged and leaned back on the bench seat, resting one arm on the backstop.

"Isn't it interesting how each of our kind so clearly offsets one another?" Yaspen stated, "Our tastes the sharpest, but we can't sniff out an enemy right under our nose."

Thavin shot him a peculiar glance. "You mean they didn't know?"

"If they had, we'd have been in quite the scrap back there," Yaspen answered.

Thavin frowned. "Why? They approved our arrival."

"I know you come from a small village in the mountains, Thavin, but in Vèspige, your kind isn't exactly... welcome.

Thankfully, those two elixirs worked as planned," Yaspen noted while refilling his drink.

"The first one didn't last very long," Thavin replied. "I felt my body change for only a few minutes."

"Well, it looks like the second one that covered your Wolven aroma carried us through the remainder of that meeting," Yaspen replied, "It also didn't hurt that your tribe has fangs before transformation," he finished, raising his glass and saluting with his cup.

Thavin nodded, his temperament unchanging.

Finishing another sip, Yaspen set his glass down and pushed the conversation forward. "Now, about my other request?"

Thavin held up a finger – asking for a moment – then removed a map from a rectangular leather satchel at his feet.

He placed it on the knee-height table between them. "I tracked that woman – the one you call Tassia – back to a cave by the Bellairs edge ocean," he finished, pointing to a location with an X written on it.

"Did you set the markings and leave that piece of mask we made?" Yaspen inquired.

"Of course," Thavin answered. As he traced his finger on the map, a blue line appeared, following it. "Every fourth tree, like you said. It will lead him right to their hideout."

Yaspen smiled, rubbing his tongue to a missing fang-stump absentmindedly. Once Davion found that little piece of hunting mask Thavin left behind – previously painted in Tassia's markings – the magic tracking salve it was covered in would lead him to Thavin's discovery.

"Unfortunately, someone was guarding the prisoner you were talking about earlier," Thavin said.

Yaspen waved him off. "Leave that to Davion. We're not in the business of saving people. Once these Houses finish devouring each other, we can secure the rest of what you found there."

"Do you really think they will attack each other so easily? It seemed everyone we met rallied together," Thavin replied before filling his glass with rum, then downing it in one gulp.

Yaspen leaned back, crossing one ankle over his knee. "That's surface level, Thavin. You see, they'll have to deal with trying to answer a rumor with no truth behind it. When I first met Carneth, he was simply a talented swordsman who'd bit off more than he could chew. Now..." Yaspen gestured his glass towards a window, "They believe he's a hired hand from the inside. By the time the dust settles on this feud between Davion and Fiona, there'll be half as many Houses left."

Thavin placed his cup back on the table and reached into his satchel again, retrieving a flask.

"Mine not aged enough for you, Thavin? Maybe I'll toss a few hides into the barrel next time," Yaspen said, smiling sardonically.

The burly man took a long pull, then sighed in relief. "I need a kick in the face to get me back up. I'm still coming down after those two potions."

"Well, that may not be the last time you have to take them," Yaspen advised.

Thavin raised an eyebrow quizzically.

Yaspen shrugged. "Partly to test their properties. And secondly, because I'm afraid we'll have to speak with the Baron again at some point. Thankfully, not anytime soon."

"Why does he have such contempt for you?" Thavin asked, "I know you were banished – I've seen those scars. But you were convicted of a minor crime. I can't imagine that small indiscretion would carry such a grudge."

Yaspen looked out a window currently being pelted with heavy rain. "It was a malignant rumor that left a boulder of hatred chained to his heart."

"And what rumor was that?" Thavin asked, eyes narrowing.

"Word spread through the Court that I slept with his wife…"

Thavin bowed his head, slowly shaking it. "I wish I knew that before we arrived…" he said, running a meaty palm through his hearty black hair, "I'm surprised he didn't snap your neck."

Yaspen rolled his eyes after another sip of rum. "It was only a rumor…"

Thavin met his eyes with an unconvinced stare.

Yaspen laughed. "Oh, calm down, Thavin. I swear, you Wolven get so worked up about the tiniest hint of broken loyalty," he turned his eyes back to the window, pointing a thumb behind himself, "With our kind, political angling and betrayal are simply how we greet one another."

CHAPTER
TWENTY-TWO

HE PRESSED HIS back to the cave wall, perking an ear at what was being said around the corner.

"If it weren't for the masks, I'd toss you into the ocean already!" Adelina exclaimed.

The piece of hunting mask he'd found at Peregrine's home had led him to a remote cave. One he happened to find Adelina prowling around. After slinking in behind her, he took refuge in a shadowy cutout so she wouldn't spot him.

'I knew the masks were too powerful to be crafted by a Vampire. I wonder who they've captured to do their bidding?' Davion noted, *'Unfortunately, I don't have time to stay and investigate here any longer.'*

From what he gathered after eavesdropping on their conversation, Carneth had escaped. Hopefully, he wasn't too far, and even more importantly, he needed to find him before Adelina. Davion waited for her to shout again, giving him a mantle that covered the sound of his footsteps. Reaching the surface, he eyed his options, then took off in one direction, hoping it was the correct one.

"If that woman hadn't blindfolded me, I'd have found Davion's place by now," Carneth grumbled, trudging through the green muck.

He wasn't sure exactly how long he'd been trapped in that cave, but he believed his imprisonment was several days at least. Sludging through another muck pile, he understood why very few traversed this section of Moncroix.

"I wish I could leap around the treetops like Davion," Carneth complained, staring at the vast limbs several stories above, "But I know Tassia didn't lug me the entire way all by herself. There must be a carriage trail somewhere."

After another mile of sloshing through ankle-deep puddles and teal marsh grass, he finally found one. A wide path comprised of pebbles and stable dirt. As his boots reached it, he sighed in relief. After miles of grime and swamp water, returning to firm footing wrapped him in a sensation of luxurious calm. Like a warm fur blanket.

His state of comfort was broken, hearing footsteps squelch behind him. Spinning on his heel, he was greeted by a murky-looking man two yards away. This was no sentient being, though. Its body was a slab of dangling pale-green skin, bulging orange eyes, and limbs so decrepit they appeared to be dripping off the body.

'A swamp-ghoul,' Carneth surmised, unsheathing his thin sword.

The gangly creature lumbered forward awkwardly, hands outstretched. Carneth took one stride forward, plunging his sword through its chest. He twisted his blade and sent a foot into its chest, shattering the stone-turned ghoul into a pile of scattered remnants. Scanning his surroundings, he noticed more ghouls clumsily shambling toward him. He easily felled them with quick stabs and twists of his weapon.

"The magic of this blade is quite helpful, father," he said, converting another ghoul into a sickly-looking statue.

He ducked a bony limb that swung for his skull. Too close to get a clear stab, he shoved a shoulder into its gut, sending the creature tumbling head over heels. Carneth stalked forward for the easy kill, but his movement halted as another ghoul grabbed his knee with both rotting arms. He smacked its face with the base of his sword's hilt. Unfazed, it continued clinging. Then it began climbing up his side, using his body to pull itself from the mud.

"Get off me!" Carneth yelled while stabbing his sword skyward to activate its flames.

He swung low and set the ghoul ablaze. Howling, it released its grip. Sliding in with one quick step, he thrust the point of his sword through the ghoul's head, leaving it hissing and bubbling, melting into a pile of steaming grime.

A thought crossed his mind. *'Are these individual beasts, or is this section of swamp actually alive?!'*

The idea chilled him to his core. Turning away from the muck and attempting to run down the path, he was greeted by a small pack of them. Stepping back carefully, he noticed a few dark brown ones mixed in with the green.

'I hope that's just a change of attire. I'd hate to find ones with unique abilities,' he thought, reaching into his back-satchel, *'No better time to try one than now.'*

He uncorked one of Ahman's Snare potions he stole from the cave and downed it, hoping it would do something for him despite not being tethered to the Spirits. He grimaced at the awful taste and waited. Nothing happened.

"Damn... At least these things move at slug speed," he said thankfully, retreating slowly.

"I'll need a new strateg..." he was cut off by a sudden pang in his head.

Brilliant red light snatched his vision as his consciousness was yanked down a pitch-black pit. The falling stopped in an instant, and his eyes met a misty monstrosity constructed with crimson smoke. It reached for him gently with claw-like fingers.

"Your call?" the Spirit asked, hovering just inches from him.

Staring in horrific awe at the scale of it, Carneth couldn't speak. The hand alone was larger than his own body, and its entire misty frame was at least three stories tall.

It leaned close to him, the face made of fog generated narrowing eyes that intently examined him.

"Your sign is fraudulent, the work of another," it said in a thin whisper, "I'll give you a taste of our power for the effort... for a cost," it said menacingly.

Carneth's eyes snapped open, returned to his former state. He quickly hunkered down, ready to defend himself as several ghouls sloppily lurched forward.

'What was all that?' he thought, panting as he tried to regain his composure.

Suddenly, he was hit with a wave of immense strength. As it pulsed through his body, he looked down at his hands, which had an outline of red smoke emanating from them.

"My prayers were answered," he said aloud, retaking a fighting stance.

He bellowed harshly and leaped towards the ghouls, sword raised overhead. His blade sliced through the first ghoul's head effortlessly. The creature wailed hollowly as it turned to stone. Clasping the hilt with both hands, he swung the beast attached to his sword like an oversized mallet, ripping several ghouls' torsos from their legs as he hit them. Yanking his sword free, he continued his momentum and lopped off another's head with a twisting strike.

The Spirit's gift of power coursed through his veins. He wasn't sure how or why, but he'd thank the god-being later. Blocking his exit on the roadway were at least fifty more slobbering monsters.

He smiled. Letting them come for him.

He charged forward – shoulder first – plowing through the pile. His violent charge scattered the hoard, bowling them over or hurling them airborne.

After storming through the first group, he was greeted by another – but much smaller – cluster of them.

'I should make the most of this,' he thought, staring at his hands, still glowing red around their edges.

His next moments of movement were like a vicious whirlwind. Effortless, rapid, ferocious. He stabbed and slashed through the mangy creatures with dizzying speed. Not even bothering to turn them into stone. Relishing every chance to keep hacking them instead. As the last one in front of him fell, eviscerated, Carneth turned back on the path, looking for another challenger. A trail of orange-eyed corpses and blanched-green sludge was all that greeted his rapacious gaze.

His fight over – but wishing it wasn't – he turned and strode down the gravel roadway, leaving the monsters behind.

Then a better idea hit him. He raised his eyes to a branch at least one story above, a speculative smile crossing his face. Soon, he was leaping from branch to branch, taking the route only someone Snared could.

'I could get used to this,' he thought, *'if it wasn't for the idea of tying my very soul to one of those Spirits, I'd have gotten one already.'*

He was arrested in mid-flight moments later as the strength seemed to seep from his pores. A soggy flaccidity crawled through his muscles. Dizziness overtook him, and he stumbled after hitting the next branch. He somersaulted down into a shrub patch, then rolled onto the path, the wind knocked out of him. Gasping, he clawed his way to a tree stump, using it to climb limply to his knees.

"I hope this isn't permanent," he panted weakly, leaning on the stump's smooth top. Quickly glancing about, he didn't see anything threatening nearby.

"Thank the Gods," he said, laboriously drawing breath through stinging lungs.

'Or at least, thank that red misty one...' he told himself.

He wanted to get back on his feet, but they were like numb sandbags. How long had he been granted power? Would it take the same amount of time to heal in kind? Was that the cost the spirit spoke of?

The weight of exhaustion slowly dissipating, he reached into his bag and rummaged for something to eat.

'This will have to do,' he thought, retrieving an apple. It was the only bit of provision left inside the bag.

'Considering it was likely one of the Vampire's, I'm lucky this isn't a hunk of raw flesh.'

He took a pitifully small bite and chewed it lazily. Getting even a slight amount of food down felt fantastic. Strength returning, he gobbled several more bites, pulp and juice dripping down his chin. Finishing the delicious fruit, he gave a grateful sigh and pulled himself up just enough to sit on the stump, arms resting on his knees.

A loud crack – like a whip – broke his pleasant rest. A beefy amphibian with shimmering sapphire skin stood a quarter mile away. Its stumpy front legs were planted on a small tree it had trampled. As it lumbered in his direction, Carneth noticed its rear legs were curved and lengthier. By his estimation, it was at least half the size of Davion's cottage.

"A giant toad?!" Carneth cursed under his breath.

He staggered upright and backed into a more deeply wooded section, hoping the trees would shield him from the wart-covered brute. He heard the cacophony of snapping and sloshing as the enormous toad shuffled through the marsh-wood, cracking fallen logs and shrubbery beneath it.

Stumbling forward, he braced himself against a tree to keep from tumbling into the dirt. Another look over his shoulder confirmed it was only ten feet away. Grasping for his hilt, he unsheathed his sword and thrust it above, hoping the flames might frighten it. His sword refused to ignite. The usual green lines were barely visible, soft, and translucent rather than lit with their usual vivid brilliance.

'This is the real cost,' Carneth thought.

His sword's Snare stolen, he limped away, the snap of the toad's tongue lashing the ferns behind him.

"Just a bit further," he muttered, hobbling behind another tree.

His breaths quickened, and his heart pounded in his chest, begging for reprieve. The stout, slimy reptile gave him none. He couldn't wait. He pushed off the tree with his heeled boot, trying his best to run. Another tongue snap made him wince and misstep. His body thumped hard against the earth. Rolling onto his back, he saw it approaching with its deliberate gait. The thin tongue darted for his stomach, but Carneth timed a perfect stab. Yanking his sword back, the corpulent toad's tongue split around it. Green blood spurted from the newly delivered wound.

"Run, or I'll do more than split it in two!" Carneth yelled, fear cracking his voice.

It screeched loudly in pain, then shrieked angrily as sets of gills flared on either side of its face. Carneth rolled away just before it slammed down a three-toed foot that looked like a giant cloven hoof. Having missed, the toad-beast used its head like a battering ram, clobbering Carneth's side and sending him a foot off the ground. He smacked down in the dirt path and rolled a few feet before slamming into a downed tree.

"Grrrah!" Carneth rasped as sharp pain punched through his ribs.

Taking a few weighty steps, it loomed over him. He could feel the humid steam of its fetid breath. Frantically searching the dirt for his sword, he panicked at the realization that he'd lost it after being headbutted by the disgusting thing. The gigantic toad reared back onto its haunches, raising both fore feet to crush him. Carneth raised an arm overhead in a futile protective gesture.

Thunk!

Somehow still alive, Carneth peered through one slit eyelid. A double-sided axe was driven between the titanic creature's eyes. Davion – standing on its head – yanked his blade free, lofted it overhead, and swung down again. Another crack rang through the woods as Davion split its skull. He jumped from the toad's back as it toppled over, gargling a death croak. Its elongated tongue hung from its mouth like a butchered eel. Davion landed gracefully on a bent knee next to it.

"What took you so long..." Carneth said wearily, clutching his broken ribs.

Davion laughed, extending a hand for the downed swordsman. "You're the one who ran away."

Carneth waved off his companion. "I...I don't think I'm ready to stand yet," he said through clenched teeth, leaning his head against the log behind him.

Davion knelt beside him and touched his side.

"Hands off!" Carneth yelped.

Opening a hip pouch, Davion dug through it. "If we're camping here tonight, I'll need to douse the area in some aromatics to ward off other hungry pests."

"Any chance there's medicine hiding in that purse of yours?" Carneth asked.

"I think there's something that'll work," Davion answered.

As Carneth blinked some of the pain away, he noticed something odd. The sun was still out.

"How are you alive in the daylight?" he asked in shock.

"This is a location desired by the Witches and Warlocks for a reason," Davion answered, rubbing a salve on his fingertips, "something in this swamp, whether it be the fog or trees, seems to keep everything concealed from the elements. Have you noticed that despite it being winter, this place is completely unaffected?"

Carneth choked out acknowledgment as Davion lifted a corner of his shirt to apply the salve.

"Gaaaah!" Carneth howled, painful heat singeing his skin.

"I guess I should've warned you," Davion said quietly.

Carneth yanked his shirt down, guarding himself against any further treatment. Davion, finished with his work, rose to his feet and briskly walked away. Carneth peered around the fallen beast, trying to see what he was up to. A minute later, Davion returned with his sword.

"I'm not sure it'll do much good out here," Carneth stated, pulling himself to a seated position. He inhaled to test his ribs, which felt better for the moment, then finished his thought. "I finally downed one of those potions. Sadly, it stole the last bit of magic my father left me."

Davion crossed his arms, frowning in confusion while observing Carneth, wondering how he held such an even tone despite the gravity of his loss. *'He's still suffering the effects of battle,'* Davion thought, knowing Carneth would show his true feelings after resting.

He set the sword next to him. "How did your weapon lose its power?"

Carneth bowed his head and laughed, exhaustion still ruling his emotions. "Go sprinkle your spices around, and I can explain after. I need a moment to collect myself."

CHAPTER
TWENTY-THREE

ONE ARM DRAPED over his bent knee, Carneth sat on his hip in front of the campfire. The flames danced between orange and yellow, providing comfortable warmth. The swamp was foggy and humid during the day, but the night brought a chill he hadn't expected.

"I thought we were protected from the elements here?" Carneth inquired.

Davion leaned forward, poking the firewood with a large stick. "We are. Maybe that Spirit sapped a bit more than your sword's magic?"

That thought had come to him earlier. He was completely feeble after using all the energy given to him by the crimson Spirit. Davion believed it was Varkin, the Spirit of power. Carneth wasn't entirely convinced. He'd grown up being taught that each of the Spirits was a colossal entity standing taller than any building. Their human-like bodies constructed from solid materials, not smoke and mist.

Yet, Ahman's words crept into his mind. *'They don't seem to be whole anymore…'*

He'd told Davion about Ahman, about the construction of the masks and potions, about everything he'd encountered while kidnapped. Davion wasn't convinced of Ahman's other-realm, godly claims, but he did believe the brawny, marbled creature could be credited with their creation.

"If Varkin stole your Snare," Davion said, breaking Carneth's thoughts, "There's a chance you could retrieve it."

Carneth turned onto his other hip, holding his still-tender ribs. "I don't see how you can steal something like that back?"

Davion shrugged. "There are people on this Intercontinent who understand the Spirits and their magic beyond anything we know. We shouldn't give up. We could visit Pere…" he trailed off before uttering his fallen friend's name. Quickly glancing at the flames, he concentrated on their dance to avoid thinking of her.

Carneth bit his lower lip and sighed. "It looks like we both lost the last piece of our former selves," he said softly, "I'm sorry, Davion."

Davion rubbed his face with one hand, wiping away his grief. He leaned away from the cold emptiness, steering his heart towards the boiling heat of frustration. He wouldn't wallow any longer. Carneth observed Davion's blank stare curl into a scowl.

"Davion," Carneth said, interrupting his friend's mental wanderings, "I can tell you're gearing up for a fight over there, but I need you to save that energy for a bit."

Davion eyes darted to Carneth. "The salve hasn't fully taken?" he asked.

Carneth shook his head. "I think I need a few more hours for my ribs to fully set. I'm still feeling the effects after drinking that potion."

Davion pressed a tongue to one fang, considering his words. Carneth had told him earlier about how Ahman had created a fake Snare. Davion and Carneth had assumed before that it merely masked an existing one.

"I'm still trying to understand how you were brought before one of them, even if it was only your subconscious?" Davion wondered aloud, "You just downed a vial with no ritual or formal prayer."

"Well, didn't you see a Spirit when you were originally Snared?" Carneth asked.

Davion nodded. "I did, but mine didn't speak to me. The other Waywards who informed me of their experience didn't have one like yours either."

"But they saw something mist-like?" Carneth asked.

Davion gave a quick head tilt. "Some did. I'm sure if you were given greater power, the process might appear differently. I wouldn't know anything beyond what my friends told me, as our kind in the Court doesn't share the origins of their turn."

Carneth squinted. "You say that like you're one of them…"

Davion swallowed the lump in his throat, physically manifesting the desire to retract his previous words. He coughed, retaking his composure. "I've lived amongst them for so long… it's taken part of my identity," he admitted.

Carneth leaned back to his other side and dug through Davion's satchel between them. After retrieving something, he tossed it to him.

Davion caught it with one hand. "A piece of smoked fish?" he said inquisitively, watching Carneth take a bite from another strip himself.

"I think you should do something human. Remind yourself who's really beneath those fangs," Carneth replied with a sarcastic smile.

Davion grinned begrudgingly and took a bite. Meat with all its blood sapped. Not exactly the most delicious thing in his currently altered form, but his enhanced taste savored the bite nonetheless.

"I don't think the potion evaporates over time," Carneth stated.

Davion raised a brow, intrigued.

"That mark you carry is an eternal bond," Carneth continued after finishing another bite, "It can sense you tampering with it. And once it eventually finds you... it steals the false one."

Davion reflexively sat upright. "What brought you to that hypothesis?"

"My father," he answered, pointing the last bit of food at him. "I know you were told that you are honor bound to leave if your Snare is broken, but that's not the real reason."

Davion frowned at the young man's dissertation. Perturbed at his flippant rejection of everything he'd told Carneth after their first encounter.

"And how do you know better than our order?" Davion replied.

Carneth looked him dead in the eyes. "When my father left, he decided to try and stay. For his family. But it's not honor that made him run off to Malcozé to build a new life for us. He was chased by the Spirits; they came for his soul. Whatever perversion that leader of yours could accomplish with the Snare was never intended. Breaking it was supposed to strike you down so you could join that Spirit. Returning the power you were given. A gift for a gift. Thankfully, they can't reach beyond Moncroix. Yet, due to my father's skill set being mercenary work, he got himself killed before we could join him there."

"I'm sorry…" Davion replied sincerely. "Once we finish this, we can seek vengeance for him."

Carneth didn't answer, looking away while chewing the last bite. After a moment of contemplation, he shook his head. "I promised my mother I wouldn't chase that killer. Eventually, she'll relent on that oath, but I won't break it until she gives me permission."

Davion exhaled his tension. "I understand."

Carneth grabbed a canteen, downing a swig of water before turning his attention back to Davion. "There's something I need to ask you. I thought it wouldn't be right when we first met, but now that we're about to march into the lion's den, I'd like to know."

Davion perked and ear. "What is it?"

Carneth bit his lip, then eventually spoke. "I want to know how you were the only Wayward to survive?"

Davion looked away, hanging his head shamefully. After several minutes of absolute silence, he returned his stare across the fire to Carneth. "Fine, I'll tell you…"

TEN YEARS
AGO

THE GALA AT House Malnuvious was quite the spectacle. Above the attendees were several candles resting in metal holders that floated twenty feet above. Beyond the candlelight, the castle's ceiling rose to a magnificent archway, painted with a scene involving every familial member. Glancing down from the impressive artwork, Davion noticed thick velvet drapes lining tall, slender windows. Perfect for blocking out sunlight. Davion surprised himself by taking to the transition into a nocturnal lifestyle with significant ease.

"Can I refill your drink, sir?" a slim attendant asked.

Davion smiled and nodded thankfully. He needed the wine, as he hadn't adjusted to the bloodthirst yet.

He gulped down his glass and then held it out again. "Could I please have one more?"

The servant eyed him disdainfully. "You must be one of the new ones..." he answered while acquiescing to Davion's request.

Davion winced. "Sorry, I've never had such a decadent way of quelling my thirst. I'm used to scouring the streets at night."

The servant tilted his chin upward. "We'll carry you out of that life," he replied confidently.

Davion bowed his head thankfully, humbly holding his cup in two hands as a show of gratitude. The servant nodded in kind, then took to assisting another guest. Over time, he and the other Waywards had slowly filed into the Royal ranks. Trying their best to join every House. They'd succeeded at infiltrating all but one, House Mayjere.

Its matriarch, Countess Fiona, possessed a shrewdness for newcomers that none of them were able to overcome. It was only a small setback since they'd finally gotten every member inside the other Houses. This was the first gala since that achievement. However, having to maintain their cover, they couldn't interact enough to celebrate, despite many of them being together this evening.

Davion took a deep breath to steady himself. He was technically one of the newer Vampires adopted into House Viruticus, but he'd been there for almost eight months now. He couldn't allow another behavioral slip like the one he had earlier. Thankfully, this gala was to celebrate the arrival of the newest member of House Malnuvious and was Davion's first visit to their manor. He followed a small crowd of Royals past the large antechamber into the banquet hall. This room also held the exquisite standards this class of Moncroix monster expected. Entering the open rectangular threshold, he passed a group of violinists serenading their gathering. A few feet beyond him were several tables lined with a variety of treats.

'Hopefully, these are infused with blood, too,' he thought hungrily.

He struggled to feast on live humans, but thankfully this Royal class always stocked a bevy of food already mixed with the precious red liquid. When joining the Royal Vampiric Court, the Waywards swore to feast on criminals and other monsters whenever they could. Leaving innocent humans as a last resort. It was an excruciating oath to hold, as they all underestimated the gut-churning desire to sink their elongated fangs into pulsing veins, which human blood cured best.

Davion took a small white plate from a stack and began selecting a few different baked goods. Unfortunately, he couldn't tell exactly how the items would taste until he took a bite, as his new skin deadened his sense of smell. His hearing, however, was incredibly adept. He tried listening in to nearby conversations, hoping there was someone worth sitting next to. They didn't have any leads so far on the potion since their leader, Gerine Leathe, discovered at least one of the Houses was working on something capable of masking their Snare. The implications of creating something that lasted longer than their initial concoction – which only gave the Vampires a few minutes of disguise – would mean the entirety of their Intercontinent could be overrun by this Royal collective.

The Witch, Peregrine, had somehow reverse-engineered it to make their human Snares evolve into Vampiric ones, but even her creation was only temporary. He was surprised she could do such things with spellcraft. The original potion itself was supposedly crafted by another Witch, but they hadn't been able to confirm if that was true. Peregrine was contacted by another sister of her coven, who only shared what she was asked

209

to improve upon. Despite multiple attempts, Peregrine wouldn't disclose which Witch came to her or the one requesting that woman's services. Covens held no duty of loyalty to keep their recipes secret but swore off selling out their buyers.

'Stubborn old hag,' Davion grumbled internally.

"Are you too embarrassed to join me, newcomer?" a voice asked him.

Davion spun on his heel and was greeted by an old friend.

"Celiss, you're here too?" Davion replied with a smile.

"Everyone is," Celiss said before taking a sip of wine.

Davion walked away from the treat tables, taking a seat at one of the circular dining ones.

Celiss followed suit, taking a seat next to him. "Don't you find it odd that everyone has been invited?"

Davion shrugged. "Considering the status of House Malnuvious, wouldn't everyone feel obligated to join?"

"Of course, many of the Counts and Countesses would feel compelled, but they don't usually have their hunters at their hip," Celiss replied, nodding to a table behind Davion.

Davion quickly peeked over his shoulder, noticing a slender woman in trim clothing wearing a hunting mask. She stood next to another beautiful Vampire, whose exquisite attire made her stand out, even amongst all the other well-dressed attendees.

"Don't stare too long," Celiss interrupted. "You don't want to catch their attention."

"I'm guessing the hooded one with the mask isn't the Countess," Davion replied, smirking.

Celiss gave a stressful sigh, eyes narrowing. "You may be one of the most skilled in our order, Davion, but stay clear of Tassia. Many of the Royals even fear her. Countess Fiona usually has her stay behind at gatherings like these because of her ruthless reputation."

Davion took another brief look at the two women; this was the first time he'd actually seen Countess Fiona in person. Her striking appearance matched her reputation. He noticed that the servants were giving Tassia a wide birth. Choosing to approach the Countess instead of the hunter.

He returned his eyes to Celiss. "I appreciate the tip, but we should save discussing these details for a less public forum."

Celiss looked away, waving one hand. "I guess you're right. I just find it peculiar that we've all been called to this induction. I haven't seen any before with attendance to this scale."

"Those two additional months before I joined make you a savvy veteran of the Court, eh?" Davion asked sarcastically.

Celiss rolled his eyes and laughed. "Alright, I see your point. Just watch yourself tonight. I've heard things in my House."

Davion licked his lower lip and squinted. "Such as…"

Celiss leaned close, carefully looking around before speaking. "Word from our Count is that House Malnuvious is on shaky footing with Baron Elbourne."

"He is the next in line and the second most powerful behind them. Don't all these Houses quarrel with the closest ones?" Davion answered casually.

His friend shook his head, taking another sip of wine. "It just seems odd to have this grand event for one induction."

211

"It's fine. Our House is just as lavish," Davion said after finishing the last bite of a raspberry blood-tart.

Celiss leaned back in his seat. "Maybe as lavish, but not with this level of attendance."

Davion extended one of his treats to his friend. "Take one. It'll calm your nerves."

A sly smile crested one corner of his mouth as he took it. Taking a bite, he closed his eyes and sighed. "You just can't beat that flavor."

"Not until we're done wearing these," Davion replied while raising half of his upper lip, exposing a fang.

Celiss nodded in agreement as he took another bite.

"Done wearing what?" a feminine voice interrupted.

They looked over their shoulders as a young lady Vampire with lengthy blonde hair took a seat across from them. Her dress had exposed shoulders and elbow-length sleeves, with maroon fabric that tightly fit around her waist and bust line.

"Viscountess Adelina," Celiss said, rising from his seat and extending his hand across the table.

She gave him hers, which he brought to his lips, gently kissing the top of it. Davion stood and completed the same formality. As she leaned forward, her dress revealed a bit more than her collarbone. He noticed her formal dress also had a set of large black bows at her hips. Her clothing seemed to find multiple creative ways to draw someone's gaze beneath eye level.

"Who's this one, Celiss?" she asked, eyeing Davion.

"This is Davion. I wanted to get to know him since he's new to House Malnuvious," Celiss replied.

Celiss was quite accomplished at schmoozing, easily procuring the names and stations of everyone he met. And most importantly, being memorable himself. Celiss was quickly gaining the trust of everyone he interacted with. Davion hadn't quite mastered this art of infiltration yet. He missed the days before, when a hearty swing of his axe resolved matters instead of idle chit-chat.

"Good to meet you, Davion," Adelina said, smiling.

"You as well, Viscountess," he replied warmly.

The ring of a brass bell interrupted their pleasantries, instructing them that the procession would begin. A few more joined the three of them at their table. Inductions always had open seating, encouraging guests to mingle.

Baron Elbourne glided past them, as their table was only one row away from the stage. Tonight, he was draped in a robe of silver and red, his black crown perched perfectly atop his head. Davion glanced at his friend, who seemed uneasy at the idea that this procession would be introduced by the highest-ranking Vampire. Unlike some of the lesser stationed Houses, which only had raised platforms one step higher than their gathering halls, Malnuvious Manor had an entire stage.

Standing at its center, Baron Elbourne waved a bony hand to one side, motioning for someone beyond the curtains. Two large Vampires covered in black-leather armor fitted with brass buttons marched forward. Each held a silver axe in one hand, their other grasping the arm of what Davion assumed to be a prisoner. The guardsmen shoved the man forward, causing him to fall to his knees. Hood covering his head, all that could be heard was soft whimpering. Murmuring clattered from the attendees as they moved in their seats, hoping to get a better glimpse. It wasn't uncommon for Vampires to feast on live humans, but that wasn't how the formalities usually started.

"We have traitors among us," Baron Elbourne stated frankly, getting straight to his intentions, "Hathric Malnuvious, join my side."

Count Hathric Malnuvious sat upright, blinking rapidly, completely taken aback by everything before him. Being called by his name without a formal prefix was not a good sign.

"This is not a request, Hathric," Baron Elbourne commanded in a harsh, piercing tone.

Hathric uneasily rose from his chair, carefully making his way to the stage. He gingerly took the five steps up, the creak of each one being the only sound emanating throughout the now deathly silent audience.

"Baron, I'm unsure what this is?" he asked, voice quavering.

Baron Elbourne pointed to the prisoner, and one of the guardsmen removed his hood. A few from Hathric's own House gasped. It was their newest induction and the last Wayward to join the Court.

'Nathaniel,' Davion thought, observing the scars covering his arms, *'what have they done to you?'*

He was dressed in a tattered tunic and ankle-length leather boots. Davion noticed a third of his hair missing from the top of his head and another large patch gone from his beard. Taking a closer look at his hands, Davion noticed a few fingernails and strips of skin were taken as well. Vampires had a plethora of cruel torture techniques, and it appeared Nathaniel had suffered through several.

Instinctively, Davion reached for Celiss' forearm under the table, sensing him about to jump from his seat. His friend caught his eye and understood that Davion's pale stare begged him to stand down. Celiss sank back into his chair, staring at the table with a hollow expression.

"Your newest recruit is not our kind, but a human masquerading as one," Baron Elbourne began, "Did you intend to tell me why?"

Malnuvious swallowed, trying to gulp down the terror blockading his vocal cords. "I…"

"I'll tell you why!" the Baron snapped, whipping forward in a blur to meet his face. "You wanted my seat to rule our Court, so you gave him this," as the Baron finished, he retrieved a vial from a small chest-height pocket. He held it aloft for everyone to witness, "You made a potion that let outsiders into our midst. And not just any human," Baron Elbourne continued, pointing to Nathaniel. "After questioning this man, I've discovered he's one of those vagabonds that slay our kind in the Midland."

"A Wayward? How…" Count Malnuvious croaked.

"Don't feign ignorance to me, Hathric! There's more of his kind in this very room, seated at these tables. Downing the same elixir to sneak themselves in," he raised a pointed finger at Hathric, lengthy claw just an inch from his eye.

"The p…potion was meant to sneak us beyond the wall," Hathric stammered, "I never intended for humans to use it against us."

"I'm glad you're willing to admit your culpability in this treachery. Raising an army of imposters to spy on our Houses so you could enshrine yourself as king," he rumbled, eyes slit in deep hatred, "Now for your punishme…"

"Baron, there's more you should know," Hathric blurted out.

215

Baron Elbourne paused, giving the Count more rope to hang himself with.

"I have another!" a feminine voice shrieked from her seat.

Davion whipped around to see a tall, red-haired Countess pointing to a husky male Vampire, who had been grabbed on either side by two men wearing similar garb to the guardsmen on stage.

Davion glanced back at Celiss, confused. *He's not one of ours,'* Davion thought, *'He must be a political enemy...'*

"How many more of them are in your ranks, Hathric?!" Countess Fiona cursed at him.

Hathric started upright, dumbfounded at the accusation, unable to respond.

"Another from your house!" Baron Elbourne yelled in a menacing tone. He pointed at the Vampire, who was trying to break free from the two guardsmen's tight grip. Countess Fiona snatched underneath his jaw and squeezed, showing Hathric's subordinate's fangs, which were shrinking to human teeth.

"Slaughter him," Baron Elbourne commanded. "Then find the rest. None shall leave this room until every one of these rats is snuffed out!"

Chaos engulfed the hall like a bursting flame. Royal Vampires whipped through the air, each one searching for anyone not of their kind. Davion ducked as one whirled overhead towards the stage. Turning quickly, he noticed it was one of their own order – Vampiric powers still intact – rushing to save Nathaniel. The Baron slashed him with a backhand, sending the Wayward tumbling across the stage. Rushing in a cloud of black and purple smoke, the Baron snatched the man's neck in one

216

hand, then ripped his head free from his shoulders with the other. All in one motion.

Davion's eyes bulged, aghast at the ease with which the Baron killed him. He turned his attention back to Hathric, who looked in horror as the Vampire ruler stalked closer, covered with drops of spattered blood. Screams rang out behind him as Vampires found more of his companions. He was watching as one took a silver stake through his skull. Davion rushed to a nearby wall, doing so with his enhanced Vampiric motion, ensuring his cover remained by avoiding human movement.

He continued darting about as the others did, eventually finding an opportunity to get involved. He rushed forward towards one of his own, knocking into another Vampire who had the same intention. He did this a few more times when the openings arrived, hoping his intentional clumsiness would give them a chance to escape.

Fighting back was futile.

There weren't enough of Davion's order present to defeat a threat of this magnitude. Hundreds of Vampires swirling and slashing, chomping limbs and eviscerating anyone believed a Wayward or belonging to House Malnuvious.

He spiraled down, cloak whipping about his body in a cloud, touching down on bent knee before shoulder shoving two Waywards. It appeared as an attack to those unaware of his true origin, but he'd saved them from a fate of snapped bones and shredded skin. Over his shoulder, he saw two of his compatriots attacking Adelina and another Vampire with silver daggers. The two men opposite the Vampires had their backs to a large, stained-glass window. Having cover behind them, they'd been able to mount a real defense. One of them ducked a blow from

Adelina and slashed her abdomen. The Viscountess recoiled on being struck with the silver blade, falling backward.

'I'll snatch Erik and Varkas, taking the three of us through the window,' Davion decided, *'giving them room to flee while I appear to save her.'*

His momentum was immediately sent sideways as someone tackled him. They went careening across a few round dining tables, shattering glassware and scattering silverware about. They slammed into a wall, causing a stone statue to tip over on its pedestal. Davion and his attacker rolled away as it fell, crashing onto the floor.

He scrambled to his feet and was met again by another charging attack. Putting his hands up, he caught the aggressor early enough to twist his own body away from the wall behind them. They whirled in a mixture of smoke and fabric, landing on the stage. Davion got up again but felt the bearhug around his waist once more, this time sending them side-stage. Their momentum shoved them through a set of double doors – which blew off their hinges – leading to a hallway behind the curtain.

Davion panted while frantically shoving his pursuer away. He rolled off his back and sprung to his feet, readying himself. His eyes grew wide at finally seeing who attacked him.

"Celiss…?" Davion started.

His friend immediately leaped for him, knocking them both to the floor.

Now face to face, Celiss whisper-shouted to his ally. "My potion will wear off soon. One of us needs to survive this."

"I'm not fighting you, Celiss!" Davion hissed under his breath.

"Someone has to complete our mission. It can't be for nothing," his friend retorted.

Davion struck Celiss's chest, sending him flying. He exhaled in shock at how much the blow had affected his friend. Celiss slowly pulled himself onto all fours and then leaned back on both knees, clutching his ribs with one arm. He could see Celiss's exhausted gasps for air that his fangs were no longer present.

"Celiss, I..." Davion started.

Celiss held up a hand to silence any forthcoming apology, then reached inside his cloak and retrieved a silver stake.

Davion shook his head. "There's another way..."

Celiss ran forward, using the last of his strength to charge Davion, a shiny spike raised to strike. Davion dipped away from the first downward slash, then ducked under another horizontal one. He continued to use his superior speed to evade his friend's assault. Davion staggered backward away from the next move, baiting Celiss in.

When the next attack came, Davion caught his friend's wrist. He stared Celiss dead in the eyes, then nodded to a window behind them. Celiss shook his head, brow furrowed. He pushed his hand even harder against Davion's grip, driving the stake closer. Celiss's gesture suggesting his plan to die would serve better than Davion's idea to flee.

Davion yelled in anger, slapping Celiss across the face. The strike sent him thudding to the marble floor. Rolling onto one hip, Celiss began laughing. He looked up at his longtime friend, his teeth now stained red as blood filled his mouth.

"After everything we've been through, and my dying wish is greeted with a slap?" he said between fits of fatigued laughter.

Davion gulped back his anger and knelt down. "Come with me, and we can regroup. I'm sure others will find us."

Celiss exhaled in relief, grabbing his friend's shoulder. He accepted Davion's assistance in helping him up.

Then he struck.

Stabbing Davion's shoulder with the glinting silver weapon. Davion howled and ripped it free. Celiss tossed a powder in his direction and stalked forward, another stake in hand. The powder hit the side of Davion's face. He screamed as the skin on his cheek and around his eye began bubbling.

An accidental whiff of it singed the insides of his nostrils. He turned onto his stomach and lept away, trying to create distance. Tears streamed down his face, his eyes stinging with the aftereffects of being dowsed in garlic powder. He felt a rush of wind and fabric overhead as another Vampire raced down the hallway past him. It slashed at Celiss, who ducked the blow and tossed more powder into its eyes. The creature wheezed as it hit the ground and tumbled into a nearby wall. Celiss slammed a knee into its chest and shoved the stake through its head.

Taking a couple deep breaths, he climbed to his feet and stalked towards Davion again. His eyes still hazy with garlic-induced tears, Davion swatted blindly with extended claws at his friend. Hoping he could keep Celiss off him to buy enough time to regain his vision. Celiss easily sidestepped his strikes and dove for him.

Davion barely dodged the incoming blow – aimed for his head. Eyes still blurry, his Vampiric lunge was mistimed. His legs connected with a stone bench, sending him toppling over. He slid across the marble, back smacking into the opposite wall. He put his hands up to catch Celiss's arm before he could stab him again.

The two continued to struggle on the ground, fighting for control as the stake drew closer to Davion's eye. Celiss may have lost Vampiric powers, but he still possessed incredible strength from his human Snare.

"Stop this!" Davion shouted.

"You'll live on, Davion. One of us has to," Celiss replied through gritted teeth.

"Dammit, Celiss, enough of this foolishness!" he yelled back.

Davion yanked his wrist free and swiped a claw at him. Celiss ducked his chin, narrowly evading the blow, then chomped his teeth into Davion's wounded shoulder. Davion yelled and responded on pure instinct, sinking his own teeth into Celiss's neck.

Nothing could stop him now.

The taste of freshly pumping blood, extracted with his own fangs, was like drinking indulgence itself. As if the two elongated teeth tasted every flavor he desired. It was like nothing he'd ever felt before. He continued to suck and slurp, unable to pull himself free from the most delicious meal in existence.

Then it was done.

He blinked, noticing his eyes no longer watered. Moving his mouth, he realized his skin had healed. Touching his shoulder gingerly, he found the former stab wound was sealed. Looking to his side, he saw his worst fears realized. Celiss lay next to him, limp and lifeless, eyes vacantly staring at the ceiling. Somehow his mouth had curved into a slight smile. He couldn't know if that was from Celiss's happiness at succeeding or the magic of his fangs, as they were known to send victims into a joyful trance.

"That's the one!" a voice accused, barreling through the hallway.

It was Baron Elbourne.

"That bastard took one from my House!" he declared angrily.

The slender ruler raced past Davion and snatched Celiss's body by the lapels. He raised the soulless vessel that once held Davion's best friend.

"You killed him?!" the Baron inquired hastily, face turned towards Davion.

Mouth dry with shock from what just transpired, Davion could only nod. The Vampire ruler turned his attention back to the dead eyes of the corpse he still held.

"You stole one of my heirs, you vile rat!" Baron Elbourne shouted, violently shaking Celiss.

As he did, limbs bumbled around like an unwieldy marionette. Finally satisfied, he stopped his violent tirade and tossed Celiss away, sending his body crashing through a nearby window.

The Baron stared down his nose at Davion, still seated on the floor. "You did well," he said flatly, then looked to one of his guardsmen, "Help this one back to the antechamber. I'm sure it took a great toll dealing with that wretched one, considering he was able to murder a member of my family."

Baron Elbourne whirled away in a cloud of smoke, too infuriated to employ his usual graceful glide. Davion felt a hearty grip under his arm, and the beefy guard yanked him to his feet.

He put up a hand, signaling he was fine. The guard's grip released. He took a few deep breaths, then stared over his shoulder at the last place he'd ever see his friend alive again.

CHAPTER TWENTY-FOUR

LEAVING BEHIND THE swamp's fog, the two travelers raised their hoods to avoid the light, pattering rain. Few drops made it through the dense cropping of evergreen trees, but hiking in the dead of night added a harsh chill to them they both wished to avoid.

"Is that why you suspected Fiona?" Carneth asked, holding his cloak tightly against his chest. Making his best effort to ward off the crisp climate, "You believe she used a potion on that Vampire sitting next to her?"

Davion nodded. "Yes. I didn't see him ingest anything, so I couldn't be sure what happened. But after seeing those needlepoint vials you took from her cave, I finally know how she did it."

There was at least another mile until they reached the carriage Davion had taken. He'd left it behind, not risking driving it through the dangerous swamp.

"Is there a chance you suspect any other Houses?" Carneth asked. "Clearly, she's played her hand, but is there a chance anyone else is assisting her in keeping that stash secret?"

Davion didn't respond. He was weary of questioning and planning. He believed Carneth's optimistic curiosity was – in sincerity – a distraction from the ample tension created after Davion revealed his story of survival. He glanced over his shoulder at the silver and black-haired boy marching behind him, a small torch raised to light his steps.

"She's kept every House far away from her secrets for many years. I believe she's solely in control of everything back there," Davion stated.

Carneth stopped and sighed, lowering his torch slightly. "I know this isn't what you wish to hear, but in the end, I believe your friend Celiss was right..."

Davion lowered his head and inhaled a labored breath, then turned to face Carneth. He bit his lower lip tightly to keep himself silent.

Carneth observed the dour expression of his friend and took a moment to choose his words carefully. "You may view yourself as a coward for surviving, but you both made a sacrifice that day. Celiss, his life, and you – your freedom."

Davion's lips curled downward into a regretful grimace. "And what does the sum of those costs equal now?"

Carneth stepped forward, poking Davion's chest, "If none of you survived, I wouldn't be given this chance to commemorate my father, and those parasites hunkering in their castles would never face justice."

Davion lifted his head, a swirling pit of raw emotions gnawing his guts. He stood firm and stared down Carneth. "I

225

appreciate this little speech, but no matter how you try and rationalize his decision, know that my best friend's blood will always stain my hands. It's something that can never be wiped clean."

Carneth squinted, considering Davion's even-toned reply. He decided to counter Davion's reasoning with a story of his own. "I always felt guilty that I couldn't do anything to save my father. That is until I realized there's other ways I can carry on his legacy," he unsheathed his sword and held it before Davion, flames from his torch bathing it in warm light.

"I took swordsmanship to not only honor him but secretly use his wisdom on those that would try to harm me," he sheathed his sword and held up a clenched fist. "You told me Celiss was the craftiest fighter you ever knew. Take what he taught you and use it against them. Don't defeat them yourself, Davion. Let Celiss join you in this fight."

Despite his best resistance, Davion couldn't help the sliver of a grin coming forth. "Your youthful enthusiasm is fairly motivating," he answered through the half-smile.

Carneth leaned his head to one side, smiling. "If it got you to smile, then I'd say it's more than fairly."

Davion huffed and turned away, continuing their hike uphill. "Alright then, let's finish what we started."

"Ah, I see Davion's leading the charge again," Fiona noted aloud while taking her seat amongst the other House leaders.

They'd been summoned to a special assembly by the Baron, claiming a final decision would be reached. Behind Davion, sitting on his elevated throne, sat Baron Elbourne. Quietly surveying everything.

"I've been given command of this investigation, and I've reached my conclusion," Davion started.

Fiona arrogantly raised her finger. "Where's the prisoner then?"

"He was in your stash of masks and potions at the cave near Bellairs Ocean," Davion coolly replied, "Thankfully, he's now secure in this very castle. Waiting to face his sentence after I disclose the culprit."

Fiona laughed, unfazed by his accusation. "I assumed you would place your ill-fated blame on me. However, you've trotted your dirty little hooves somewhere you're not allowed, Davion. Yes, I have a place there, just as you have yours near the swamp Peregrine calls home. If none of you are familiar," she gently waved an upright palm to everyone, beckoning them to listen, "she's the Witch responsible for making Malnuvious' potion," she pointed a finger at Davion, "The one you're so obsessed with."

He shook his head in disappointment. "You can't squirm free this time, Fiona. I have proof, which the Baron has seen for himself. Carneth finally admitted to being complicit in front of our leader."

Fiona leaned back, crossing her arms. "How convenient. You just happen to find him in the perfect place at the perfect time. But let me ask you something," she said, retrieving a small vial from a coin purse resting on the table in front of her. She held the vial for all to see. "Tassia uncovered this when she did a bit of investigating for me. Does this seal look familiar?"

Davion leaned on the table, moving closer to inspect what Fiona was holding. "I'm afraid I don't know it?" he lied.

"Somehow, I don't believe that..." Fiona retorted smugly, handing the vial to another Count seated next to her. "Please share that with whichever record keeper is present," she requested cordially, "If he's unfamiliar with the seal, I'm sure one of our House members waiting for us in the gathering hall next door should be able to verify my claims."

Count Rifteal nodded and rose from his seat. He waved to a stocky man, wearing a tight leather vest with gold buttons, a white long-sleeved shirt, and pinstriped black trousers, who was seated behind a table with pen and paper in front of him. The record keeper of House Elbourne hurriedly rushed from his chair to retrieve the vial. House Elbourne, being the one to host the meeting, was the only one allowed to have anyone beneath a level of Count present. Anyone else brought along had to wait in a separate chamber.

Lifting a monocle from his front vest pocket, Darius Elbourne inspected the seal. He was only the second recordkeeper in their House's history. The position was highly coveted by the Baron and not given flippantly. His House being the highest ranking in the Courts, they had an incredibly vast knowledge of everyone that traded wares in Moncroix. It would be a surprise to anyone present if he didn't know who the markings on the glass belonged to.

While he inspected it, Fiona continued, "I remember the last time we sat here, you had a letter from Yaspen and Peregrine. Either by a stroke of luck or insidious cunning, you never read that letter from her, did you?" she gestured to the other members gathered at the table, "At least not in front of us."

"This seal is hers!" Darius excitedly interrupted.

Davion swallowed back a lump of anxious frustration, hiding all emotion as he planned his next verbal joust. Even though he knew Peregrine never placed her seal on the vials of potion given to him, the truth didn't change the impact of her maneuver.

'I'm guessing she had that creature forge Peregrine's seal on it,' Davion thought as he recalled Carneth's description of the one Fiona employed to make the hunting masks.

He pointed to the vial in Darius' hand. "Presenting a vial with her seal does nothing to discredit my argument. I only communicated with her to find clues in connection with the killing, same as I did with Yaspen. I can retrieve the letter if the Counts require it, but a slip of parchment won't twist your guilt back onto me."

Her eyes narrowed as she leaned forward, casually resting her forearms on the table. "I'm curious what the Baron thinks about you being able to find this elusive killer all by yourself – twice might I add – without a single scratch to show for it," she placed a finger on her chin, "I think you used Carneth to try and uncover how I make my hunting masks because you and your House wish to steal that piece of industry from me."

"I DON'T CARE ABOUT YOUR DAMNED MASKS!" Geldam roared.

He glared at her, eyes red with bitter rage, and both hands pressed firmly to the table as he leaned forward. "Unlike many of the Vampires that join our Houses, Thadric was my actual flesh and blood," he continued, slamming a fist on the table, "I think you'd find a bit stronger urge for revenge in your heart if someone killed your little brat, Adelina, compared to an adopted member," he tilted his chin up and crossed his arms, looking down his nose at her, "Then again, I don't know if an icy bitch like you would care at all."

Fiona's eyes widened with contempt and anger. She started to speak, but Geldam cut her off. "We can squabble here for hours, bandying accusations until we all croak," he said, then pointed to the Baron, "However, if neither of us proves to be overwhelmingly true, Baron Elbourne will raze both our Houses to the dirt."

Fiona scowled. "And what do you propose then?"

Geldam reached into the front pocket of his overcoat. He slammed a silver-colored coin on the table. It was constructed of Kratasian chrome, one of the strongest metals in all the Intercontinents. Etched into the coin was a tusked hippoar's skull with two large swords behind it, the seal of House Viruticus.

"I demand trial by combat," he growled.

Worried murmuring ensued as everyone else discussed the implications in hushed tones.

"Enough," Baron Elbourne snapped, commanding silence. He looked at Geldam. "You understand the consequences of going through with this?"

Geldam pointed to Fiona. "The only way I'll get justice for Thadric is to destroy the House responsible. If we can't win, then I have no place ruling a part of this Court anymore."

'What is he doing?' Davion wondered in complete disbelief. He knew with a bit more time and a few select reveals of proof along the way, he could convince the Counts and Baron Elbourne to rule in his favor. Now, however, his entire plan was laid in the hands of a battle between two chosen warriors. One to represent each House. Something he had no control over.

"Having made the declaration, Geldam," Baron Elbourne said, "You must choose your representative first."

Geldam pointed to the head of the table. "I choose the best Hunter I've ever employed. The one who's caught you in every lie you've spun, Fiona. I choose Davion!"

The skin around Fiona's eyes wrinkled as her face broke into a wide smile. "If you wish to place the survival of your entire House in his hands, then I pity you."

She turned in her seat, waving a female servant over. The tall woman elegantly strode to her. She wore a white, sleeveless peplum dress trimmed with black edges. Her contoured attire, ruffled at the waist, and thin features, invested her with a prim, classic look. A perfect example of the House that employed her.

As she arrived by Fiona's side, she was beckoned even closer. The servant obliged Fiona's second request, leaning forward to receive whispered instructions into her perked ear. She nodded in acknowledgment as Fiona patted her shoulder, then left the room. Fiona clasped her hands calmly on the table, casually eyeing the other attendees while they waited in excruciating silence.

Suddenly the doors opened, and the female servant returned. Two house servants kept them open for a slender figure, cloaked and hooded, a hunting mask concealing her face.

"I choose Tassia to represent our House," Fiona finally answered.

CHAPTER TWENTY-FIVE

"I THINK THIS is the best plan we have," Davion stated.

"You said that the last time I was stuck behind bars," Carneth chided.

Davion rolled his eyes, turning from him. "I know you'd rather be out there hacking away at them, but this requires a finer touch."

"I just don't see how you can land a sneaky move like that on Tassia," Carneth replied, grabbing a piece of dried meat from the plate of rations Davion brought him.

Davion shrugged. "I have to make the most of what we've been given. This fight with her is something I hadn't accounted for. But after mulling it over, I believe it actually gives us a better chance to leave this castle with both our heads attached."

Carneth finished his chewy bite, then spoke. "After you beat Tassia and all those Vampires descend on Fiona's House, I know you need to come back and get me. However, if you get the chance to kill Fiona yourself along the way, I'll happily wait."

Davion hissed a quick laugh. "If I get the chance, I'll take it."

Carneth swallowed another tough bite of meat. "That's the spirit. Remember, she's the one who killed all your friends. Including Celiss…"

Davion took a deep breath, biting his lip. Finally, he nodded in agreement. "Yes... she is responsible. Even your father's death rests at her feet."

Carneth raised an eyebrow, tilting his head. "I guess you could pin it all back on her. Maybe if she hadn't lured everyone in with that potion, I might have become a Wayward myself. I think if given the chance, we'd fight pretty well together."

Davion's eyes narrowed. "Maybe..."

Carneth smiled and saluted Davion. "Let's find out when this is over."

Davion slowly entered the stone archway onto the arena floor. Crescent rows of seating occupying both ends of the rectangular floor were filled with everyone able to attend. The Court wanted to eliminate any opportunity for interference, so anyone from the involved Houses was forbidden to attend, including the rulers themselves. Once a House's combatant perished, the surviving competitor would lead the charge to begin a complete slaughter of the other house.

Davion surveyed the towering grey block walls on either side of him. Standing atop them were more onlookers who didn't have the status to get an interior seat. Scrolling his eyes down, he noticed the windows inset every few feet just above his own height, marking hallways used to circumnavigate the building.

'I might have a better chance if I use our environment against her,' he thought.

Nothing forbid the fight from taking itself beyond the flat arena floor, as long as it stayed inside the castle grounds.

Davion looked to the spires beyond the arena proper, additional ideas swirling in his mind on how to deal with Tassia. The large set of stone structures comprising Castle Vèspige was ungoverned by any specific Royal entity. It was the only neutral site in the entire Court. Remaining empty until it was needed to host specific occasions. A fight deciding the fate of an entire House was easily considered worthy of occupying its quarters.

Davion eyed the circular entrance opposite his own, watching the still darkness. Waiting for his opponent to arrive. He took one last look above, gazing at the violet moonlit sky, littered with white stars. It was the first day of winter he'd been able to see them, as rain clouds had concealed their presence for the last few months. It was nearly spring. A time for life to emerge anew.

Davion drew his eyes back to the archway, reminding himself of the opportunity that lay before him. To finally escape the city of Vèspige and its Vampiric Court. If he survived... no, when he survived, he could leave this life behind him to evaporate under a drench of sunlight. Like a block of ice left out in scorching heat. He'd regain his humanity, never to consume that wretched potion again.

The chattering crowd hushed as Tassia strode through the opposite entrance, daggers sheathed on her hips. Davion touched the hilt of the axe strapped to his back – anxiously ensuring it was still in place – and strode forward. There was a red oval platform raised at the floor's center. A short, thin woman, hair pulled tightly back in a bun, extended her arm for Davion. He stepped onto the raised surface to join the officiant.

She approached him, wearing full armor to protect herself from any accidental injuries. It consisted of a silver breastplate for her torso, and leather armor dipped in a melted version of the same metal on her legs. She had several stakes – made of silver as well – placed into a leather holster strapped onto her hip. She also wore a helmet with a grilled face covering, which was hinged and currently raised to better speak with the fighters.

"This battle must stay within these grounds. If you leave them – willingly or not – it will be considered a forfeit," she instructed, pointing to the farthest visible castle spire beyond the unroofed arena, "You may only use the weaponry on your person. If I see you take something from anyone in this crowd, it will also be a forfeit," she continued, pointing towards the stands, "You may use any means you wish to dispose of your opponent within this castle that's unassisted," she finished.

Davion gave a solitary nod of acknowledgment.

She nodded back and continued. "Any decision I make or judgment I give is final. Tonight, there is no one present from either House to politic or sway me. This fight will only end in surrender or death. Any final questions?"

He silently shook his head no. Having no further instructions, she turned away and approached Tassia to provide the same guidance.

He eyed Tassia, inspecting her gear and weaponry. She wore her dark-blue contouring bodysuit that fit snuggly against her slender frame. Its fabric had a smooth yet lightly stubbled texture, like velvet. Her hands were covered by leather gloves of the same color. Observing her waist, he spied her sheaths. The daggers within seemed thick and rectangular, like a cleaver with an added point on top. However, the light divots in the leather near the sharp end showed a possibility the blades were serrated.

236

He noticed a hip pouch on one side, the size of two hands, which likely held potions and small weaponry. He didn't notice anything strapped to her back, but her boots sported tiny hilts on either side.

'*They're likely stakes,*' Davion told himself.

She still wore her hunting mask to conceal her face. Davion knew she was never seen without it, so he brought his own as well. Wearing it was the only way – at least to his knowledge – that someone could see through their projections. Most of House Mayjere wore masks mirroring human faces accented with shimmering gold. Elegant and poised. Hers didn't subscribe to their customary colors, however. It had a smooth white base emblazoned with slashes of maroon paint. Like blood splatter on marble. Its shape was a mixture between a jackal and a wolf. Menacing and vicious.

Having fully looked her over, Davion noticed the trim-fitting bodysuit topped by her threatening facial covering was an impeccable mixture of beauty and aggression. Her projection of the perfect predator complete at all times.

Rolling his shoulders and twisting his neck, he shed the tense preoccupation and stomach-wringing trepidation that he'd brought to the arena. He needed to rely on instincts now. Built from years of training, stretching well beyond his time hunting for House Viruticus. If he was to defeat the most notorious Vampire in Moncroix, he couldn't allow any sliver of doubt to crawl in.

The officiant stepped back to her previous position to Davion's right, centered between them. She lowered the face covering of her helmet, which gave her head the appearance of a metal crow.

237

She looked at Davion, pushing her arm out, palm flat and thumb tucked. He saluted approvingly. She made the same motion to Tassia, who turned her head and nodded in kind.

"COMBATANTS…" she boomed. Her voice – enhanced by the helmet's embedded magic – echoed from the floor to the arena stands beyond. Raucous cheers rang out as the crowd's baited anticipation would finally be met with battle.

"BEGIN!"

CHAPTER
TWENTY-SIX

TASSIA YANKED HER pointed cleavers from their sheathes, dashing forward. Davion whirled sideways in a whip of violet smoke, dodging her incoming attack. He left his double-sided axe strapped tightly to his back, letting her strike first so he could gauge her offense.

'*She attacks in ravenous flurries like a starved hound,*' he thought.

She levied another barrage of furious swipes with her dual cleavers, causing him to leap backward. His boots skidded to a stop on the stone floor beyond the smooth platform.

His eyes narrowed on her. '*Let's use that thirst for violence against her.*'

He jumped forward in a high arc, landing with his feet atop one of the wall's deep-brown window frames. She growled and raced after him, thinking he meant to scale the wall and flee. As she lept, Davion feigned a surprised expression. Tassia descended from her vault, arms outstretched, readying her bony, textured blades for crossing slashes. It gave her the appearance of a crocodile's jaw preparing to devour its next meal.

Seeing her close in, he pushed off the wall, arms overhead and fists clenched. He spiraled into her like an arrow made of purple and black vapor. His fists connected with her chest at the halfway point of her swing, sending them both tumbling to the hard surface below. Tassia twisted herself mid-air, knocking herself free from his grip.

They both thudded to the stone floor, then rolled a few feet in opposite directions. Davion scraped his claws on the stone to halt his momentum, whipping himself up to one knee. He looked forward and saw Tassia in the same position. It was a common technique for Vampires skilled in combat.

He noticed her hands were empty, then glanced to his left and saw the glow of her etched stone blades lying on the ground. They both jumped for them. He timed his leap to land after she did, sending his shoulder into her side. She flew back, smacking shoulder first into a wall beneath a section of seating – the crowd gasping as she hit. He looked down to scoop up the blades, but they were gone... He instinctively ducked as another swipe came for his head.

'How did she manage to snatch the blades and keep hold of them,' he thought while flipping backward to create distance, *'I hit her with all my strength.'*

Davion knew he'd have to use his axe soon. He could only evade for so long without something to block or strike back.

'I just need a location better suited for my weaponry,' he thought, looking to one of the nearby windows.

Behind it was a hallway. The narrower environment would favor him compared to the open area they stood in now.

He circled her, positioning himself in front of a window. She stalked towards him at a measured pace, understanding he was angling himself strategically.

'Of course, she's careful now...' he grumbled under his breath.

He crept away from the window as she closed in, her mask projecting the face of a snarling, white wolf with bright eyes, exhaling faint whisps of blue breath. As he reached behind his back to grab his axe, Tassia took the opening and darted forward.

Behind her mask, Tassia's eyes grew wide as Davion dove into her, wrapping her waist in a bear hug. He dove for the window, glass shattering as he sent them both through it. High-pitched laughter emanated from the watching audience.

Now inside the hallway, he climbed to his feet and snatched his axe. Tassia got up slowly, watching him as she rose from the scattered glass. Straightening herself, she tilted her chin upward, staring down her nose at him. Davion gripped his weapon's hilt tightly, eyes unwavering as he studied her.

"I was waiting for you to finally challenge me," she said slyly, pointing her cleaver at his weapon.

She hunched as she spoke, readying her next strike. Running forward, she jumped and twisted her body, spiraling for him like a bladed whirlwind. Davion swung his large dual-sided axe in an upward arc. She stopped her spinning and crossed her arms, catching his weapon between hers. Her momentum continued as she pushed off the swing, flipping overhead. Landing behind him, she mule kicked one foot into his spine, sending him sprawling to the floor. He was barely able to hold onto his weapon as the sting of a thousand needles stabbed his back.

Sensing her nearby, he gritted through the pain and rolled to one hip, swinging his axe in a wide arc. Her advance was halted by the blow, and she stopped her charge. Her boot heels dug into the stone as she skid across the floor. Howling in anger, she increased her mask's wolf-face projection to the size of a boulder. Davion quickly threw his own mask on. It consisted of two short horns, narrow eye slits, and short spikes running in a vertical line from the forehead to chin. It was painted a mixture of swirling black and chrome. Wearing it allowed him to see through Tassia's projections. Now she'd be unable to create any meaningful distractions.

She ran towards him again, and Davion swung his axe for her heels. She skipped over the blow easily, tucking her knees to her chest. Now mid-air, she swooped for his unguarded body, readying another cross strike. He yanked his weapon's long hilt back to himself and caught it with both hands, holding it like a staff. Sparks flew as her glowing bone blades smacked the steel handle. He gasped as one of her knees landed on his stomach. She held it there and flipped her blades into an overhand grip, then plunged them downward. He turned his weapon handle in his hands, trying to put the sides of his axe blade between himself and her pointed cleavers.

"Yaaaaagh!" he screamed as she stabbed his ribs.

He'd only been able to block one.

She leaned forward and twisted the knife, a greedy smile hidden beneath her mask as she tortured him.

"Try to run from me now, Davion," she hissed.

He dropped his axe and snatched both her wrists, stopping her from stabbing deeper. He twisted in vain, trying to shove her off, but her knee held firm against his belly. Teeth clenched and eyes watering from impaled agony, he tried his best to regain enough sense to think of an escape.

'Carneth's tactic...' he thought in an instant, eyes wide from discovery.

He kicked his knee into the leg holding him down, shoving her forward, then pushed her wrists up. The move sent her tumbling overhead, and she landed hard on her back. He let go of her wrists and snatched his axe, then took off in a wisping jump to put several feet between them. Tassia got up and stared him down, noticing the area she'd cut was closing as he downed an elixir.

"How many of those did Peregrine give you?" she teased.

"Enough to keep me standing until this axe is lodged between your eyeballs," he retorted.

Laughing at his response, she nodded to his waist. Davion's brow furrowed in confusion; then he felt something dripping near his left side.

'The wound didn't fully seal!?' he worried frantically, noticing it still oozed blood, *'What monster corpse did she plunder to craft those cleavers?'*

He reached for another vile, but she hampered him by lunging forward with an overhead slash. He dipped to one side, rolling away from her, then crouched in a defensive stance near a window. She dove in with another furious assault. The force of her swings made it hard to keep his axe aloft to stop them. Vibrating surges of pain coursed through his arms with every block.

243

Frustrated at not feeling her cleaver connect with flesh, Tassia spun on one foot and kicked Davion in the chest, sending him careening through a window on the opposite side of the flat arena floor.

He plummeted several yards down, landing hard on a slab of stone inlaid in the courtyard below. The crowd yelped upon seeing him fly through the glass. Everyone standing on the roof above the hallway rushed to one side, hoping to catch a better glimpse of the action.

Tassia followed him by leaping through the open window, landing on one knee gracefully. She watched as he pulled himself to his knees, axe scraping the ground as he drew his weapon close. She rushed in, spiraling towards him in a whirling cloud of red smoke. Her blades struck his upright axe, shoving him across the courtyard.

"If you keep this up, I'm afraid I'll have to break your little toy there, Davion," she said mockingly.

He groaned in exhaustion, pushing the top of his blade against the ground. Using the weapon like a cane to reach his feet. Finally upright, he searched his pouch again, looking for a second elixir. Not willing to let him heal, Tassia shoved her blades into her sheaths and rushed forward, snatching his groping hand in hers. In one swift motion, she yanked his leather pouch free with her other hand and threw it. From the corner of his eye, he watched it sail over a high wall that led to grounds beyond the castle. Grounds he wouldn't be allowed to enter unless he wished to forfeit.

"No more tricks, Davion," she hissed.

He returned her threat with a sly smile. "I'm afraid I can't oblige, Tassia."

He lifted his axe and slammed it into the ground. Green shockwaves sprang from it and ripped apart the grass and stone beneath their feet. The wave of magic sent Tassia flying into a castle wall. A surprised roar came from the onlookers standing on a walkway atop the same wall.

Davion unsnapped a pocket on his leg and grabbed one of only two vials he had remaining. The last one contained something even more important than his final healing potion, which is why he'd kept it on his person.

Tassia laid on one side, hand holding her head, trying to get her bearings after being sent skull first into the stone. He took a deep breath, noticing the pain was down to a solid ache, and the wound had stopped weeping.

"You're mine now," he snarled behind his mask, which projected the image of a roaring lion.

He charged in, swinging his axe for her neck.

She caught the blow at the last second, barely getting her blades in front of it. He clasped the highest point of the axhandle with both hands, shoving it down against her. She grimaced while shakily holding her weapons against the force of his weight. Unable to completely cave in her block, he released one hand from his weapon and swiped for her mask. She turned her face and clumsily rolled away before climbing to her feet, then defensively presented her blades. He watched her, panting as sweat dripped from his brow. The healing concoction worked like a bandage, covering the largest wound it found, but it didn't have enough additional power within to cure his fatigue. He was growing weary from the fight, even with his Vampiric enhancements.

'I can't relent now,' he said under his breath, stalking forward.

He turned his stride into a dash after seeing her reach for something, assuming it was a potion to heal herself. She ducked his horizontal swing, rolling away again and uncorking a round glass orb. She inhaled the contents in one gulp while scrambling back to her feet. Davion swung again, and she ducked once more.

'Wait for it...' he thought, timing his next move.

She spiraled forward in a gust of spinning red mist for his back.

"Now," he said, whirling on his heel, holding his axe at the base of its handle like a club.

A burst of green energy engulfed the courtyard as his spinning attack struck her with a loud crack. She'd crossed her cleavers in front of herself at the last moment – avoiding death – but not surviving the blow entirely. The momentum of his perfectly timed hammer swing sent her flying skyward over the wall, back onto the arena floor. Just like smacking a stone across a river with a bat.

Tassia gasped in pain as she viciously thudded onto the raised arena center stone. She breathed heavily, fumbling around in her hip pouch for another healing potion. Looking to her left, she saw a dark figure descending the wall and advancing on her.

"Dammit!" she cursed, scooping her blades off the ground.

It was too late.

She howled as something sharp gouged her arm. She reached over with her uninjured hand, grabbing beneath the axe blade before her attacker could yank it free to swing again. As the axe's head crackled with green light, she summoned all her

246

resolve to maintain her grip despite the sharp agony coursing through her. His opening finally revealed, Davion swept in and snatched her hunting mask.

A high-pitched jeer came from the crowd when they saw who was behind it.

"I thought you said I'd be fighting Tassia," Davion stated after revealing her true face.

The officiant swooped down from her perch with a hand raised. "We were instructed that Tassia would be the combatant. You are not allowed to compete for her…"

"I am Tassia!" Fiona snapped, whipping her head towards the judge, "I always have been…" she admitted, resorting to the truth since not doing so would disqualify her.

"So, you used stand-ins to fool us all this time?" Davion replied in an accusatory tone, waving an arm toward the audience, "What other lies are you hiding, Fiona?"

"Oh, spare me your theatrics. If it weren't for me, Vèspige would be a pile of smoldering rubble," she indignantly retorted.

"And why is that?" Baron Elbourne asked after leaping from his throne to the arena floor.

She eyed him harshly and didn't respond.

Davion took a step forward. "Because she worked with Malnuvious to make the potion and bring the Waywards in. When he planned to tell us the night they were caught, she created a distraction before he could reveal she was his partner. I'm guessing her plans to take the throne were tossed aside. At least until she employed Carneth to begin assassinating us. If Malnuvious…"

"Malnuvious was a fool!" she barked back, "He called that creature to Moncroix and wanted it to make him something to walk beyond the wall. But when it failed, he turned to me – like all of you do when you need your little messes cleaned up – and asked for my help…"

'So Malnuvious brought Ahman here…' Davion thought.

Fiona staggered, falling to one knee in exhaustion. She took a few heavy breaths before lifting her head and continuing her tirade. "He was going to keep trying until he could walk past the wall. He believed we could take over Qulàire. But I knew better. We'd never beat the Snare, nor should we. Crossing that wall would eventually mean war. A war we wouldn't win."

She grunted and pushed herself back onto both feet. "But we could take over the Midland with the right play, so I lured the Waywards in and got them all slaughtered. As for Carneth… He was never part of my plans. For all I know, he was sent by someone loyal to Malnuvious, looking for vengeance upon the rest of us."

"You expect us to believe that, Fiona?" Baron Elbourne inquired scornfully.

She huffed a brief laugh at his dour demeanor. "You turn your nose at me, Baron? Well, I built this place. Not you or anyone else in this miserable Court," she spat, gesturing a nod to the crowd seated in the stands behind him, "I created the masks, the hunting grounds, the secret control you all hold dear. But now that the truth is laid bare before you, somehow it makes me deserving of your ire?" she shook her head, "No, no, no… my accomplishments have given this place the host it needs to suck on."

"You speak of us as if we're parasites," Davion accused, bristling for effect.

"Aren't we?" she asked rhetorically, "Malnuvious mistook our kind for conquerors, but I understand our true nature. Unfortunately, every Royal here confuses themselves while sucking everything around them dry."

"Are you even one of us?" Davion asked harshly, "Or were you one of them all along?"

"A human!? Hah!" she bellowed, "Trying to cover your tracks again, Davion? How about you tell us why you…"

"Prove it," Davion demanded flatly, "Show us your Snare."

She looked to her right arm, then to Davion. Who understood she couldn't raise it due to the gaping wound in her shoulder.

"May I?" she asked snarkily through clenched teeth to Baron Elbourne, who responded with a curt nod.

Reaching her uninjured hand into her pouch, she retrieved her last healing potion and uncorked the lid, gulping it down. A rush of relief ran up her body as the wound began to sew itself together. Finally whole, she rolled her right arm a few times to knock loose the last of her pain.

"Here's your proof," she chided while presenting her right fist and turning, exposing the swirling lines that represented her unending ties to the Spirits beneath Moncroix.

The crowd recoiled in horror as her displayed Snare had no red lines swirling through, the Vampiric mark. It was the Snare of a human.

"What is this?!" Fiona exclaimed in shock.

249

Davion stepped forward, pointing at her wrist. "After discovering your hideout, I inspected your records and know how the potion conceals you. I coated my axe in a salve from your lair that unveils your true nature."

His story was a complete lie but one that served his plan perfectly. When swiping her mask, he'd also swapped the potion in her pouch with one that turned her Snare from Vampiric to human. He knew she'd have to take a healing potion to lift her arm, and luckily the Snare potion had medicinal properties as well.

'Defeated by Malnuvious' original concoction,' he thought, laughing to himself at the irony.

Fiona convulsively touched her face in horror as her fangs shrunk. She saw Davion smile while sliding a vial into his pocket.

"You switched them!" she shrieked, "You did this to me!"

"I've done nothing but expose you for who you really are," he replied, crossing his arms.

Baron Elbourne pointed at her. "Feast upon her lying soul!"

Her eyes bulging, she turned to flee. *'If I can buy enough time, it should wear off...'* she frantically thought.

Then they were upon her, swooping down from the stands in every direction. She fought them off as best she could, but they cascaded over her like an ebony wave. Taking turns tearing at her flesh and stabbing their pointed teeth into her supple skin.

Davion took a step forward, revenge fueling his decision.

Then he paused.

Another second of witnessing them feast like rabid hyenas changed his mind. Fiona, the one responsible for taking everyone he cherished, was defeated. There was no reason to participate in their games anymore. His work was finished.

'It's the fate you deserve, Fiona,' he thought, watching their greedy display of carnivorous gluttony. Each of them fought for a chance to suck a piece of her carcass dry.

He turned from their feast and left the arena. Head held high as he passed through the arched exit, knowing he was leaving the Court behind forever.

EPILOGUE

TIPPING HIS HAT brim down, Yaspen reached the end of the cave with his Wolven bodyguard in tow.

"Would you look at all of this?" he said, marveling at the stacks of masks and vials surrounding him. "It's a shame Fiona isn't around to enjoy it anymore."

He removed his hat and set it on a nearby table.

"What is that?" he asked in shock, retracting his arm after seeing the table was half covered in a pile of ashes.

Thavin leaned forward and sniffed the dusty remains.

"Ooof, I've never caught that scent before," he replied, waving a hand in front of his face, "It's as if someone doused a lemon in black pepper..." he turned away, then gave a loud sneeze.

Yaspen found a rag and brushed away the dirt, then set his hat down. He pointed to it with both hands. "It's just some dust, Thavin. You're acting like you've seen a ghost."

"Sorry, boss...." he got out before giving another hearty sneeze.

Yaspen shook his head and strode to the center of the room, mentally adding up the value of his newfound wares.

"Keep it together, Thavin. I'll need your help hauling everything back before anyone else finds this place."

❧

"The first sunrise of his next life," Davion said, pushing the small canoe from the shore.

It slowly bobbed along the water, the only thing inside being a small chest.

"Once the sun tops the horizon, I'll give you the honor of doing the rest," he said, looking over his shoulder at Carneth.

Carneth looked down at the round orb in his hands, a wax Wayward emblem pressed onto one side.

"You'll toss that firebomb to burn his last remains here," Davion instructed, pointing to the small boat, "This lake is where the founders originally met to create the Waywards. This ceremony signifies he's leaving this Intercontinent and entering the afterlife."

Carneth nodded in acknowledgment, then glanced at him. "You sure your potion has worn off? I don't want you burning up on me too?"

Davion smiled, fangs nowhere to be found. "Yes, I'm sure."

Carneth sat down on a nearby stump, carefully setting the round object away from their campfire. "Well, we have a few more minutes until sunrise, at least."

Davion found a large stone to seat himself on, then put his hands out before the flames to warm them.

"Is there part of you that feels guilty over what happened to Adelina? I know you spent a

253

lot of time with her," Carneth inquired.

Davion hung his head for a moment before replying. "I had to lay blame at her feet for your escape. It was the only believable reason I could give Geldam. Besides, we only shared a bed, not a heart. If she knew who I really was, she'd have torn out my throat without hesitation."

Carneth turned his head, looking at Davion with a raised eyebrow. "Is there anyone there you'll miss?"

Davion spluttered, not expecting that question. "Honestly, there's a few who I'd consider friends, but no one worth staying for. I'm done being a prisoner there."

"Does he expect you to bring me back?" Carneth asked.

Davion shrugged, continuing to hold his hands in front of the flames. "I told him I needed to leave Vèspige, get away from the political anglings, and disappear after everything that transpired. He won't suspect me if I don't return."

Carneth leaned his arms on his knees. "Are you still interested in removing your Snare?"

Davion tilted his head in contemplation. "I thought it would be an easy answer before I left, but it's hard to say now. I still want to visit that Wolven shaman who removed your father's Snare. I'm surprised Gerine couldn't do it himself."

Carneth shrugged. "That's what my father claimed. He said that was another secret Gerine hid from you all. He only learned the magic capable of applying one but didn't have the ability to remove it. When my father questioned him, he said every previous leader passed on the same wisdom."

Davion shook his head. "I wonder how much he hid from us?"

Carneth looked to his right, beyond the lake, and towards the horizon. A faint light peeked above it.

"It's time, Davion," he said, rising from his stump.

Davion got up from his stone seat to stand beside Carneth, who scooped the small wooden ball from the ground. He took a few quick steps forward before hurling the object overhead. It hit the boat with a burst of red fire. They stood and watched the fire consume the small vessel, burning it away from their world.

"If you keep your Snare, is there any chance you revive the order?" Carneth asked, still watching the dancing blaze.

Davion shook his head. "When those flames extinguish, so do the last remains of the Wayward order itself," he glanced at Carneth, "Were you hoping I could help you become one, like your father?"

Carneth uttered a brief sigh. "It crossed my mind."

"You've already accomplished more than most of them," Davion replied, firmly patting his shoulder, "The Waywards may be finished, but that doesn't mean we can't build something new."

AFTERWORD

Thank you for reading my third novel, hopefully you enjoyed your trek through Moncroix. While this story is complete, it won't be the last time you see Davion or Carneth. I have more adventures planned for them in the future. If you enjoyed this tale, please leave me a review on whatever platform you purchased this from. If you would like to remain up to date on new releases, please visit my website AsherNovels.com. I hope to see you soon.

- Bryan Asher